FLIGHT

Stories

AMY TEEGAN

For anyone who needs permission to leave.
Go.

Contents

Geese

Sunday morning. Sunny and bright and the gravestones cast harsh—though small—shadows as it draws closer to midday. The quiet, tranquil pocket of green invites visitors to reflect. To linger.

A flock surrounds two headstones, picking at bugs that only they can see through the blades of grass. Scuttering away when a human approaches, but otherwise loitering. Taking up space.

Give Artie My Love

Submitted into evidence for a protection order applied for by Mrs. Lauren Figueroa against Ms. Heather Estes. Transcript of a series of voice memos texted from an unrecognized number believed to be that of a burner phone Ms. Estes purchased at the Sunoco gas station nearest to Mrs. Figueroa's home. Background noises indicate the speaker was driving for the first few minutes before the car turned off. All voice memos sent over the course of four hours and forty-eight minutes.

Memo one. 11:48:02 a.m. EST

"Um . . . hi, Lauren. Hello. Yeah, I, uh . . . This is . . . um, this is Heather again? I left you a voicemail yesterday. I hope you've listened to it already. I'm just going to assume you have and, uh . . .

"Well, I mean, I've left so many voicemails, and not only have you not picked up once, but the recording has cut me off every time. I'm sure that's partly my fault."

[Laughs.]

"I probably ramble. But I wanted to make sure I gave you all the details for this invite so you can be just as excited to go as I am."

Memo two. 11:48:50 a.m. EST

"Right, but, like . . . I know. Why would you pick up, right? I mean, when I don't recognize the phone number, I don't pick up either. But I would think that you would recognize my number by now, even if you haven't saved it to your contacts yet. But, also, I had hoped you would be brave enough to have saved me into your contacts by now. I like to think that Artie wouldn't have married someone who was a coward, or who shied away from having real conversations."

Memo three. 11:49:21 a.m. EST

"I mean, that's why I looked up your phone number in the first place. Although, now that you know how easy it was for me to hunt down that information, maybe you all should look into . . . I don't know, paying for some kind of privacy protection? I mean, I only knew your husband's name and your home address, plus a guess at your birthday from a teeny bit of Facebook sleuthing, and I was able to get so many more details. I heard once that literally anyone you meet could become a stalker, so if I were you I would try to be a little safer. You know? I don't want to panic you, of course, but I wanted to let you know.

"What else are friends for, right?

"Because we *are* friends, right? I mean, even though we haven't met in person. Internet friends are real friends, too. For sure."

[Clears throat.]

"Right?"

Memo four. 11:50:12 a.m. EST

"I feel certain he must have told you about me, so it surprises me that you're not more eager to meet me and be friends. But, I guess, what do I know, right? It's not like I dated him for half of his high school years. It's not like I was his best friend and saw him through failing out of calculus and destroying all his father's big expectations for him, right? It's not like I was the one who he turned to for comfort during that biggest defining moment of his youth. Even though we haven't actually lived in the same city for, like, twelve years, that foundational relationship when we were sixteen was not nothing.

"Okay, anyway. Sorry. That's not why I was calling. It's just that getting sent to voicemail was a surprise, so now leaving you the voice memos has me all thrown off. What was I saying? What was I saying . . . um . . ."

Memo five. 11:51:06 a.m. EST

"Oh!"

[Laughs.]

"I remember now. You know when I called yesterday and left you more options for where we could meet for lunch? Since you hadn't responded to the message I left before then about getting together, I figured maybe you needed even *more* options. I'm totally flexible. Wherever you want to go is fine with me. *When*ever you want to go. I can make sure I'm available.

"Really. Just . . . call me back. Please. I promise I'll recognize your number and pick up."

[Laughs.]

Memo six. 11:51:45 a.m. EST

"Anyway! So, this morning, when I was thinking about maybe some other restaurants I could suggest, in case you don't like Italian or Thai or salads or barbecue, I went out and grabbed a copy of that city magazine. I know you've lived here for a while, so you probably know, but every month there's this magazine about the events going on here and all the small businesses, and I for one have found it essential to help me feel more at home, like I'm putting down roots after moving here and not knowing anyone but Artie.

"And you.

"But mostly Artie, which is why it has actually—"

[Laughs.]

"—hurt my feelings a bit that you haven't been more welcoming. I'm sure you have work and kids and all sorts of things filling your schedule, so I guess I understand why you haven't been able to make lunch plans with me yet, but I had hoped you might have at least called me back.

"Or that Artie might have. Or returned *one* of my texts. I mean, that guy . . .

"Okay, so, I'm sure whatever he does at the hospital is important or whatever. Those administrators get paid a bunch for a reason. But he was not just my high school boyfriend. He was my best friend and, at the time—remember, I was sixteen—I was sure he was my soul mate.

"I mean, I gave him my virginity. The least he could do is text me back."

Memo seven. 11:53:47 a.m. EST

"But, obviously, you know all this. I'm sure he must have told you. We were sixteen, yeah, but also just . . . like . . . so important in each other's lives, I imagine any conversation about his past and how he got to where he is now would not be complete without at least a mention of me. Or, like, a dozen. I mean, sure, we only lived in the same town for four years, and haven't seen each other in more than ten, but . . . still. Those were some intense four years."

Memo eight. 11:54:20 a.m. EST

"Did he ever tell you about the time that we almost got arrested? The time we were in his mom's car parked on the side of the road in the dark, making out? It was technically a private road, but that's what made it a good spot. Way fewer cars driving down it. No streetlights, even. Unfortunately, the thing about a private road is we were technically trespassing, and little did we know that one of the old men who lived there enjoyed . . . flexing his muscle, shall we say. I learned later from other friends that this guy called the police any chance he got."

Memo nine. 11:55:04 a.m. EST

"Anyway, we were . . . kissing, and touching, and starting to get undressed. My shirt and bra were both off, and Artie's pants were off already, when I was practically blinded by a flashlight beam to the face. And I froze. Oh my god, I was so scared. I totally didn't even think about covering myself up. Just my boobs hanging out for whoever this stranger was. And he—she? I don't actually remember—they knocked on the window and asked to talk to Artie, and he pulled on his pants again, and my brain clicked back on and I pulled on my clothes, and Artie stepped out of the car.

"And then, by the time I really understood what was happening, I was absolutely certain the cop was going to bring us into the station. We were so clearly kids. Perfect excuse to call our parents. But, fortunately, they just let us off with a warning. It was an inside joke with me and Artie for so long. Even now, if you ask him about 'getting caught with his pants down,' he'll probably laugh."

Memo ten. 11:56:03 a.m. EST

"You know, we must have a million stories like that. Little harmless adventures that just made us even closer. I bet, in all the years you've been with him, you've probably heard them all, right?"

[Laughs.]

"I know that if I ever married someone I'd want to hear all the stories and fun adventures from before we met. It's just interesting, you know? I know a lot of people might think it's . . . I don't know . . . unhealthy in some way? Call it 'obsessing over your partner's exes' or whatever, but I just think he was a whole person before he met you, right? Of *course* you want to know his background and what made him the way he is, right?

"Like learning what he wanted to be when he grew up, or why he chose his particular major, or family Christmas traditions, or whatever. That's all part of it. That all contributes to what makes Artie, well, Artie."

Memo eleven. 11:56:59 a.m. EST

"How long have you guys been married? I'm sure I knew at one time, but I forget. I know—"

[Laughs.]

"Artie probably expects my world to revolve around him, but in fact all I have memorized is his birthday. And parents' landline phone number. And, I guess, his current phone number, too, if I really thought about it. What are you planning for his birthday, by the way? It's only in three months, so please, *please* feel free to utilize me as best you can. I'm happy to distract him while you set up a surprise party, or I can be available for a nice dinner out with friends, or whatever you want.

"Whatever *he* wants, I guess. His birthday and all."

[Laughs.]

"What was I saying? Lunch plans? Artie growing up. Birthday . . ."

Memo twelve. 11:57:47 a.m. EST

"Oh! I remember. I picked up one of those city magazines from the place right by your work—did I mention that already?—and when I was looking through it I noticed there's a beginning yoga class at the lake park today. In an hour or so. And I know you've been meaning to work out more, right? I think I saw you post that on Facebook as one of your New Year's resolutions. And, like, I'm not a beginner, but I am happy to go with you. Maybe show you a few things. So, anyway, I thought it would be fun. If not lunch, maybe something you and I can do together to get to know each other, since we're going to be friends now that I've moved here. Maybe even a weekly thing? Plus—oh my god, it's really the cutest thing—this month a portion of all class fees is being donated to a charity for mental health something or other, and I know your mom is bipolar, right? So I thought it might be something close to your heart, you know?

"Just trying to be thoughtful. For my new best friend, am I right?"

Memo thirteen. 11:58:43 a.m. EST

"Anyway, we need to leave for the yoga class soon. Maybe stop at a deli or something for a sandwich on the way. But since you haven't called me back about the other invites, I wondered if maybe your phone isn't working for some reason, so I came over to invite you personally. Actually—"

[Laughs.]

"I just realized that if your phone isn't working, you're not going to get any of these anyway, so I'm just going to knock on your door. I've been sitting here parked on your street for a few minutes already. I'll see you soon!"

Memo fourteen. 12:09:03 p.m. EST

"Hey, um . . . do you know if your doorbell is broken? I thought I could hear it ring through the door, but maybe it doesn't sound on your second floor or wherever you are. The basement? Out back? The yoga class starts in less than an hour and it's like a ten-minute drive. I see a car in the driveway, but maybe . . . Oh well, I'll try again."

Memo fifteen. 12:17:38 p.m. EST

"Look, Lauren, I don't know why you think I'm stupid. I can see movement in your house. Not all your curtains are closed as tightly as you seem to think. I *know* you're in there and I don't understand why you're ignoring me."

[Sounds of five heavy thumps, presumably subject banging on the door.]

"Silly me, I guess, assuming it would be a *nice* thing for me to invite you out, and a *nicer* thing for me to offer to pick you up on the way there. I mean, we both know Artie isn't the most . . . observant man in the world, right? He probably isn't even bothering to find *anything* that's going on in town, just relies on you to plan all of it. He's totally that type, isn't he? Leaving all the emotional labor of the household to the wife?

"You know how many women say they know what *real* love and companionship looks like because of their female friends? That could be us. I mean, look, this first time we're going to hang out together and I made a plan and offered to buy you food, and now I'm here to make sure you don't have to worry about anything.

"But you're just *fucking* ignoring me."

Memo sixteen. 12:23:34 p.m. EST

"You know . . ."

[Long silence. Sound of breathing.]

"Maybe I should *call* Artie just to make sure you're okay. He changed his phone number recently, right? But I'm pretty sure I found the new one. And, really, I wouldn't be able to forgive myself if you had collapsed or something while I was just sitting out here in the sunshine. He probably wouldn't forgive me either. I mean, if the number of times he has blown me off in favor of spending time with you instead is any indication . . .

"Yeah, that's what I'll do. I'll call your husband. Artie will know what to do."

Memo seventeen. 12:25:02 p.m. EST

"You know, it's really immature that you're refusing to talk to me at all. I gave you *so many* chances. I left you my phone number at least . . . what, like, a dozen times? And texted, but you never responded. Not once. Not even to say you were busy or didn't like Thai food. And now I'm here, and you're here, and you're not answering the door either? What is it? You think you're too good to be friends with me just because I've been divorced a few times? I don't match your suburban perfect cookie-cutter ideal? Come the *fuck* on.

"You know, Artie must have been so embarrassed to marry you that he didn't even tell me about it until the wedding had already happened. So congrats for *that*. I guess it wouldn't surprise me if you had some kind of weird, obsessive jealousy about me."

Memo eighteen. 1:03:45 p.m. EST

[Sound of slightly labored breathing and rapid steps on pavement.]

"You called the *police*? What the fuck, Lauren? Calling Artie I might understand, but obviously he's at work right now. Can't come save you from big, bad Heather, who really was just trying to be kind to her oldest friend's wife. How dare I, right? Jesus Christ.

"They kept me for, like, thirty minutes or something, just asking what I was doing in this neighborhood, and how I knew you and Artie, and why I wasn't leaving when no one answered the door. It was so *fucking* insulting. I hope you're happy.

"And now it's too late for *me* to go to the yoga class, goddamnit. Really fucking selfish of you."

[Deep, audible sigh.]

Memo nineteen. 1:10:22 p.m. EST

[Deep, audible sigh.]

"Okay. You know what? I've taken a moment, and I've calmed down, and I realized . . . I get it. I really do. You must have a lot on your plate. Whatever it is obviously must be a factor in not returning my calls. You probably barely have time for your child or your marriage, is my guess, let alone any extra time to spend with *me*, a virtual stranger. We both know from your New Year's resolutions that you don't have time for your health. Too bad the yoga class has already started.

"Anyway, now that I've considered it more . . . honestly, I'm sorry I pushed so hard. I should have been more sensitive to what you're going through. That's my fault. And, really, if there's anything I can do to help, I hope you'll let me. I'd like you guys to feel like you can count on me. Like Artie did when he and I were together.

"Did he ever tell you about the time that he ran out of gas on his way home from an away football game? He and his friends drove separately, and this was before everyone had cell phones, so the only person he could reach was me. I had to go buy a gas can and find him in the dark, and it took hours.

"Before you ask, no, I don't know why he couldn't just walk to the closest gas station or even call Triple A. We were kids, I guess, and didn't think about it? I don't know.

But it doesn't matter, because I was happy to be there for him. Like I want to be there for *you*, if you'll let me.

"Well, anyway. I'm sorry if I made your day too stressful. I'll fix it."

Memo twenty. 1:13:19 p.m. EST

"I tried calling again, just in case, but since you're *still* not answering, I wanted to leave this voice memo here for you.

"As I was saying earlier, after leaving the cops, I'm sorry if I made your day stressful. Having to call the police was probably not what you thought you'd be doing, and for all I know I derailed your whole day.

"So . . . I thought about it, and I realized that there *is* something I can do to help your day get better. I know you'd never want to put the burden on me and so wouldn't ask, but I really don't mind. Like I said, you can count on me. Really. So I figured it'd be useful if I pick your daughter up from school. I know talking to the police could take a while, right? They said they'd be talking to you to go over the report.

"And we don't want Margo left waiting."

Memo twenty-one. 1:52:19 p.m. EST

"Oh my god, sorry I couldn't pick up your call! Oh my god, I feel so bad, after all my trying to reach you and then, when you finally call back, I'm in the school's office signing Margo out!

"I've got her now.

"It was no trouble at all, I swear. Don't even worry about it.

"It was pretty easy to guess what school she's at, since

I know your home address, and the receptionist there was shockingly gullible when it came to believing some reason why they should let *me*—not her mother—sign a first grader out of school early. Maybe it was my confidence, or just that I know so much about you guys. A well-placed comment about Artie's mom—I've known Pamela since I was thirteen—went a really long way in convincing her to let me take the girl.

"Margo was a little hesitant at first, but like I said . . . I know you guys. I know Artie's family. She and I are going to be best friends soon. And I'll bring her home later."

Memo twenty-two. 1:59:23 p.m. EST

"I'm not picking up your calls because that would not be safe to do while I'm driving, Lauren. Come on. But a voice memo I can do without getting distracted.

"You all must be real sticklers for safety. I tried to get Margo to sit in the front seat, like a big girl, but she insisted she's supposed to sit in the back. She was *real* wary about the fact that I don't have a booster seat for her. Since when do six-year-olds need a booster seat to ride in a car? Is that new?

"See, this is why I don't have kids."

Memo twenty-three. 1:59:23 p.m. EST

"All right, we're at . . ."

[Muffled noises, as though the subject is covering the microphone.]

"Just get whatever!

"Sorry, Margo interrupted me. We're getting a little

after-school treat. Apparently she got one hundred percent on a spelling quiz, and we wanted to celebrate.

"After ice cream, I'll see what else she wants to do and keep you posted. Since you've stopped trying to call me, I guess you're probably busy with something else. Hope it's fun!"

Memo twenty-four. 2:02:13 p.m. EST

"Oh, also, I just saw they're doing the yoga class again next Tuesday, if you want to go with me. I can drive."

Memo twenty-five. 2:23:23 p.m. EST

"Hey, sorry, I keep getting a ton of calls from numbers I don't recognize, and I don't know if one of them is you calling from . . . I don't know where. Margo doesn't seem to know any phone numbers for *anyone* in your family. Seems like an oversight, no? What if she's somewhere without you and needs help getting home?

"Anyway, ice cream went well, and since school doesn't end for another forty minutes, I assume you're busy. I'll hang on to her, don't worry."

Memo twenty-six. 2:43:56 p.m. EST

"Um . . . did you have them send out an Amber Alert for Margo?

"I'm trying not to worry too much. The model and color of the car is wrong, and the license plate is only a partial, but the description of Margo is pretty accurate.

"Jesus, Lauren . . .

"I won't jump to conclusions. I'll just put it out of my mind."

[Slightly manic laughter.]

"This is not my problem to worry about. If this alert *is* supposed to be for me, I assume the DMV will give the police corrected details as needed. Until then I'll just keep hanging out with your beautiful daughter. I think she likes me. I'm sure the ice cream helped."

Memo twenty-seven. 2:58:11 p.m. EST

"After all that effort to get me to answer the phone, you hang up on me?!"

Memo twenty-eight. 4:36:56 p.m. EST

[Subject's tone noticeably calmer.]

"You know . . . honestly, despite having to talk to police several times, this has actually been a really great day. It started out a little frustrating, I won't lie. But I don't blame you at all. Like I said before, I can only imagine how much you must have going on to neglect your family and your house—and, let's be honest, your front yard. We women have to stick together, and I am happy to grant you a little grace, given all of that.

"Plus, you know, it was so nice to finally meet your daughter, and to feel like I was doing something really helpful for you. When Artie and I were together we made so many big promises to each other, that we'd love each other forever, that we'd always look out for the other, and this was really the first time in a long time that I've been able to keep that promise.

"And, *of course*, to finally be able to connect on the phone with you was the highlight! It's just too bad we missed the yoga class this week. But next week I'm totally available. You just call me.

"Or I'll call you. Maybe just show up to pick you up

again? The cops did let it slip that you were home the whole time, so I guess that means you have nothing on your schedule at one p.m.?

"The only thing that could have made today better would be if the police had let me talk to you and Artie, instead of keeping me practically corralled on the street. It's really sweet that Artie came home early from work for you. I've missed him. And he's looking great!

"The cops, though . . . I tell you, they were *so* aggressive, for a minute there I thought they might try to shove me into the back of a cruiser. But I was able to talk my way out of it. It's not like I'm *dangerous*.

[Laughter.]

"I know, they were just doing their job. Follow-ups to the misunderstanding and whatnot. They seemed to appreciate that I could show them my phone records and all the times I had tried to get ahold of you. Maybe, if you had *answered* one of those times, there wouldn't have been this whole mess.

"Anyway. Tell Margo again that I'm so proud of her for the spelling test. I'll call you again next week to make plans for yoga.

"And, of course, please give Artie my love."

EXCERPT from the police report from the same:

Ms. Estes returned the child to the Figueroa home at approximately 3:10 p.m. EST. Mr. Figueroa came to the front yard to collect the child and refused to speak to Ms. Estes before returning inside. Ms. Estes was detained on the sidewalk, off of the Figueroa private property, and questioned. She denied any pre-planning of kidnapping the child and indeed showed the officer her search history on her phone to learn which school the child may attend. She also showed the officer her phone's call history, indicating the multiple attempts she made to contact the child's mother both before and during the time she had the child in captivity.

Ms. Estes was dismissed with a warning. The Figueroas were made aware of the conversation and stated at that time that they would be contacting a lawyer. No charges filed at this time.

Pastor Matt

When Pastor Matthew Atherton arrived to help lead our church youth group, we all studiously avoided talking about him for at least two weeks. Instead, it was, "Do you think everyone will be at the roller rink on Friday?" or, "Has anyone confirmed they are volunteering at the soup kitchen on Saturday?" We all knew what we were really asking, even if we were not yet brave enough to say it.

Our mothers would ask which boys would be there; our fathers would remind us to cover our shoulders. But none of that mattered, because the boy we were truly interested in was in fact the twenty-nine-year-old theology student who was getting "hands-on" experience pastoring high school kids.

Pastor Matt was introduced to us one Sunday morning in September. The school year had started a couple weeks earlier, and as part of his graduate degree he was required to volunteer two hundred hours at a church. Whatever searching and interviews that had happened before he was assigned to our youth group had been done without us ever knowing.

These were the years before cell phones, before the Internet. All we could learn about Pastor Matt was what he or the other pastors told us. He was from Kansas, but he came to Southern California to go to college because he had always wanted to be a surfer. He was the second oldest of seven children, and before he was called to be a pastor he had been in a band while selling shoes at a mall. We imagined what his younger brothers might look like, how popular he must have been when he was in high school, what his band might have sounded like.

One thing we knew without anyone telling us was he was absolutely dreamy. Jessalyn was the first of us to point out that he looked like Matt Dillon. Thick dark hair, intense eyes, an easy smile. He made us feel welcome, wanted. No matter what was going on, he always had an offer of praise or assistance. At the end of Sunday school each week, he was quick to stack the chairs, the last one out of the classroom to make sure everyone was taken care of. We feigned helplessness and confusion for a reason to interact with him, but we probably didn't have to do that; he would have gladly given whatever time we wanted and shown us his full attention.

One Sunday morning, after Pastor Matt had been with us for two and a half months—after we had admitted to each other in secret whispers how attractive he was, how much fun to be around, how charming and interesting—Jessalyn surprised us. Apparently, earlier in the week, Pastor Matt had called her at home and asked her to help set up the sanctuary for the Sunday evening service. He needed an extra set of hands, he said. Each

Sunday morning our church would fill with congregants and then would empty by noon and needed to be cleaned and set up again for that evening's event. It wasn't an enormous task, but far more than one person could do easily on their own. It made sense, Jessalyn reasoned, that Pastor Matt would ask for help.

We assumed he'd be asking all of us eventually, but that never happened.

Instead, week after week, Pastor Matt fulfilled more of his volunteer hours with high schooler Jessalyn working alongside him. Originally, she'd told us that her own volunteer hours would look good on college applications, but as the months went by she talked less and less about going to college the next fall. More and more about how much she wanted to be a mom. If any of us thought it strange, we didn't say so. How could it be inappropriate for a pastor to spend time with a member of his congregation, in a relatively public place, simply moving chairs or cleaning windows for a few hours?

When Christmas came around, the holiday service required far more preparation than Pastor Matt and Jessalyn could do on their own. Most of the youth group and many of our parents made the time the Friday night beforehand to deck the sanctuary from top to bottom. Our fathers ordered pizza, our mothers assigned tasks. Someone got on the sound system to make sure we had the constant background of Bing Crosby, Dolly Parton, Alvin and the Chipmunks for hours.

And all through the preparations, Pastor Matt held court. He had a vision of how the room should look, how he could help prepare for our head pastor's grand Christmas morning sermon. He was particular without being controlling, enthusiastic without being a clown. We in turn tried to please him, to get his attention, to call him over to see what decorations we could put up and get his approval. It was Jessalyn, however, who had his eye more than any of us. She'd told us they were becoming good friends through all their Sunday afternoons together, and we couldn't help but notice. We couldn't help but burn with private envy.

As the evening progressed, he seemed to be at Jessalyn's side more and more. One of the boys would try to flirt with her and Pastor Matt would smoothly interrupt. One of the mothers would try to enlist Jessalyn to vacuum the foyer, but Pastor Matt would insist he needed her particular eye on the festive garland and lights. We were looking for it, so we noticed the way he paid her special attention all while pretending not to.

(Later, our mothers would ask us if there was something going on there, but we could only shrug. Nothing that we could name.)

Before the night was over, we were dragged into the ladies' bathroom for a hurried, whispered conclave. Huddled together, we all watched as Jessalyn looked so happy she could cry.

"Pastor Matt gave me this for Christmas," she said shyly. She dug into her pocket and pulled out a small, black jewelry box, held open in her palm to show us.

It was a delicate gold crucifix necklace. Simple and seemingly innocuous, but far more intimate than the situation called for. Especially given that she was the only one of all of us who received a Christmas gift from Pastor Matt at all. We exclaimed and murmured, asking her what it meant, was there a card, what did he say. She demurred, shaking her head against all our questions, even as she could not stop grinning.

In spite of her clear elation, she did not put it on. She whispered to us to not tell anyone else about it, and stuffed the box back into her pocket. It would be several months yet before we would see her wearing the necklace out in the open, but by then there would be no question about what such a gift meant.

After that night, after the holidays, we saw even less of Jessalyn. Our final semester of high school began, and she was pulling further and further away. If she wasn't volunteering at church, she was at her new after-school job at a daycare. Though we couldn't recall Jessalyn ever showing so much interest in children, after the changes of the previous months, it was no longer surprising. She was singularly focused, intent on becoming the ideal Christian woman, which of course meant putting behind her all her previous dreams. College. Career. Moving to New York City.

For Jessalyn's eighteenth birthday, we had planned to surprise her by showing up outside her last class before lunch and whisking her away for the rest of the day. We had gifts, flowers, and a reservation at the one fancy(ish) Italian restaurant in our town.

But the day of her birthday, she didn't even show up to school.

Instead, we found out later that Pastor Matt had arrived at Jessalyn's house at 7:30 that morning, armed with coffee, donuts, and an oversized balloon before her parents had a chance to leave for work. By the time breakfast was over, Pastor Matt had asked their permission to date their daughter and it had been granted.

When our own parents heard this story, there were pursed lips, side-glances, and deep, steadying breaths. We heard low rumblings of heated conversations behind closed doors. But in public—at church—we only saw smiles and congratulatory offers. No one let their true feelings show. No one questioned what God may or may not have communicated to the family in answer to prayer.

The girl was eighteen. Her parents were approving. What could be done?

And so, Jessalyn spent her eighteenth birthday ditching school with her new boyfriend.

One month later they were engaged—we assumed the delay was for some illusion of propriety, to prove they were not too eager, had waited the appropriate amount of time, that they could make godly choices. Jessalyn had assured us, under much questioning, that nothing inappropriate had ever happened, that Pastor Matt was always the perfect gentleman, but we knew better than to take that as undisputed. We had seen the way he'd watched her, even doing something as mundane as straightening a row of chairs. We knew what our fathers had told us about what boys want.

Nevertheless, as soon as it was legal, they were official, and a month later engaged, with the wedding set for three months later—immediately after he was to graduate. After they *both* were to graduate, in fact, but somehow only his degree warranted planning around or even mentioning.

When Pastor Matt had first arrived at our church to work with the youth group, we had all assumed—we had all hoped—that his volunteering would be leveraged into a full-time position after he finished school. We, of course, would be graduating out of the youth group, but we would still be at church. Still see him each Sunday.

We had been wrong.

Once his two hundred hours at our church were up—the same week he got engaged—Pastor Matt was gone on Sundays at least a third of the time. Jessalyn told us he was traveling around the country, interviewing for other pastoring positions. She explained that it would be a conflict of interest for him to stay at our church, that he wouldn't command the same respect since we had all known him as a student. We supposed it made sense in theory, but we feared what it meant in practice.

Even with Pastor Matt being out of town often, we didn't get to see any more of Jessalyn. She had to fill her hope chest, she told us. She had to pick up extra shifts at work, to save money for their home. She had to learn how to cook all of his favorite meals, and there were only a couple more months to do so. Though she never admitted this specifically, we got the impression that she only barely finished her last semester of high school. The rumor was that her father threatened to not let her use the phone to talk to Pastor Matt if she did not complete her homework and attend school every day.

When we were shopping for prom dresses, Jessalyn was sewing her own wedding dress.

When we were sneaking kisses with cute boys behind the bleachers, Jessalyn was attending pre-marital counseling.

Though we could understand a crush, we could clearly see that Pastor Matt was attractive, we did not quite understand the leap from that to marriage. Not at eighteen. Not with so much we had yet to experience. But

Jessalyn insisted she was in love, that she had not wanted to go to college anyway, and that God was calling her to be a stay-at-home mother. A pastor's wife. What higher calling could there be?

And so, in June, we were bridesmaids. We were usherettes. We threw bridal showers and made questionable lingerie purchases, trying to make light of the utter seriousness of what Jessalyn was committing to. We gave readings of Bible verses and helped decorate for the reception. We did it all with smiles and excitement for our friend, never knowing it would be the last time we got to be with her.

The wedding was beautiful and emotional, as weddings are. Jessalyn's father remained stoic as he walked her down the aisle; her mother seemed to be on the verge of tears all day. We thought that perhaps the bride seemed afraid, but we chalked it up to nerves.

The day after their wedding, the new couple left for their honeymoon—a four-day weekend in San Diego. When they returned we spent another week helping her pack, though with most of the wedding gifts still unopened there was not much to do. Two weeks after the wedding, Pastor Matt got behind the wheel of a moving truck and drove Jessalyn away from us, away from her family, her community, and toward Tennessee, toward his new job as the associate pastor of a small church there.

And that was the last we heard from Jessalyn.

We tried. We didn't just give up on her. We sent letters and cards and got photos printed to stuff in big envelopes to let her know we were thinking of her. We missed her and we hoped Tennessee was beautiful. We told her about our college classes, our boyfriends. We tried calling more than once, but either we had the wrong number or the new Atherton family did not have an answering machine. Jessalyn's parents heard from her more often, but even they seemed strained when we asked about her. Apparently, by the end of summer, she was pregnant, but we never did hear an update on that.

Over time, however, we stopped trying. We had our own college experiences, our own boyfriends, heartbreak, big dreams. Most of our parents still lived in the same houses, still had the same phone numbers. She could find us again if she ever wanted to.

Much later, we found Jessalyn on Facebook. Twenty-three years had passed, and she was no longer using the last name Atherton. It seemed she had only opened her account in the last few years; there was no evidence of the intervening time. All of her photos showed Jessalyn as an adult, a mother of four girls. Taken on the first days of school, at the oldest girl's soccer game, helping the youngest paint her bedroom. There were a couple photos of Jessalyn on her own, dressed up and beaming, healthy, happy, holding some small award or certificate, evidence of her hard work and accomplishment as a real estate agent.

Pastor Matt was not in any of the photos.

Nor, it seemed, were Jessalyn's parents.

____

Closing Night

____

"Last time," she whispered, a little excited, a little sad.

Audra leaned forward to look at her face more closely in the mirror, to ensure that the line of heavy foundation was blended well enough along her jaw and neck. Glancing at the clock above the door, she realized she'd been backstage at the Atlas Theater for almost an hour already, getting ready to go onstage. It was more time than she really needed—she noted none of the other actors had arrived yet—but there was no way she was going to risk being late. Not ever, but especially not tonight. It was closing night, and there were traditions to observe. She had needed enough time to leave out the handwritten thank-you cards she'd made for each member of the cast and crew before they all arrived.

And so, Audra had shown up two hours before curtain, her Uber driver looking askance as she insisted yes, please, drop me off in this alley behind the theater long after the sun has gone down. There had been a tiny moment when she wasn't certain the door would even be unlocked this early, but then she was inside. First to sign in to the call sheet.

She would have wanted to come to the theater well before curtain regardless. After this final performance, after the cast party, she would not have another reason to come back to the theater for who knew how long. No reason to see these people. No chance to strengthen these tentative connections she had made in the industry. She wanted to spend as much time here as she could while she had the chance.

The next show the Atlas Theater had on the calendar was *One Flew Over the Cuckoo's Nest*, and though she had auditioned for the one role she could have possibly played (kind of, if you squint), Audra had not been cast. There hadn't been any announcements about the plays or musicals the theater would be putting on after that. And so, tonight could be the very last time she was backstage here. She hoped not. She'd audition for everything she possibly could. But nothing was ever certain in this business.

As the youngest of the adult cast (or oldest of the kids), Audra was already self-conscious about how she was perceived in the company. She'd arrived early enough tonight that the stage manager had teased her as he went about his own duties, asking if she was there to bring him dinner. She'd spluttered her awkward apologies before he'd reassured her that he was joking.

Maybe she should have brought food. A few large orders of french fries or something? Should she leave now, find a grocery store, and bring back another closing night treat?

But after the stage manager returned to his final

checklist, after Audra had left her small collection of sealed envelopes at each corresponding chair in the dressing rooms, she sat down at her own spot in front of the mirror for the last time. The row of bright lightbulbs around each mirror in the small dressing room behind the stage was far better than the light in her bedroom at home, and it was only when here that she felt as though she could see herself clearly.

This must be what she looked like to other people.

She turned her face from one side to the other, feeling the heat of the bulbs on her face. She closed her eyes, taking slow, deep breaths and trying to imprint this memory deep into her mind. The heat of her hot rollers made her warm all over. The costumes were a little stale, being sweat through night after night with not nearly enough time in between for laundry. The smell of hairspray still lingered from the night before. From down the hall she could hear the coffee percolating, but only the tiniest whiff reached her.

Audra loved the theater. It was such a cliché to spout off something about it being magic, but that's always what it had seemed like to her. An unreal little bubble where anything could happen. Not just what occurred onstage, but the entire system. Everyone working together. Props being exactly where they need to be. The give-and-take of emotional scenes with another person who is being just as vulnerable as you are. There was a forced intimacy in this kind of temporary community that she thrived on. Each person had their own role, both acting and behind the scenes. Being part of a theater company offered her something that she didn't have anywhere else in her life.

She clung to it now, already mourning the end of this final performance.

The door to her dressing room was propped open while she did her hair and makeup. As the hour mark drew near, she heard the heavy door to backstage open and then slam shut. Her heart leapt at this knowledge, that someone else had arrived.

The night was beginning.

She heard the light ruffling of a puffy down snow jacket being removed in the tight, heated space. She looked toward the hallway expectantly, hoping that her open door would be welcoming for whoever had just arrived.

Steps approached. Tess—an older woman who Audra idolized and a little bit feared—strode past the open door without offering her a glance, her down jacket folded over an arm. She tucked her short, black hair behind her ear and made for her own dressing room.

Audra had held her breath the whole time, willing this woman to look at her. She was maybe in her early thirties, and Audra held dear her one experience of the two of them having an actual conversation. No, it had not even been that. She had been present in the circle while *others* had a conversation with Tess. At the very first rehearsal a couple months earlier, there had been introductions, casual snacks, and drinks, all in an attempt to manufacture a quick camaraderie. Audra had heard Tess from across the rehearsal space—a raspy alto that could be sensual or motherly in turn, that pulled attention in either case.

Audra had shyly crept to the edge of the small group, each of them seeming to be working actors trading grievances. One had lately worked at a haunted house for the spooky season. Another spent her Saturdays dressed as various technicolor characters for children's parties.

"Oh *god*, that sounds like a nightmare," Tess had said with a laugh, her eyes shifting to Audra, who was the youngest of the group by at least six or seven years. "I'm so glad I get to do my job alone from home. No sticky fingers or crying. Except my own." She chuckled and took a drink.

Audra leaned forward eagerly. She still had only the vaguest idea how to make a living as an actor and wanted to soak in all the wisdom she could.

"What is it you do?" one of the men had asked Tess, a hint of defensiveness in his tone.

"Voice actor. Mostly audiobook narration, but you could also book me on Fiverr if you need a podcast intro." She rolled her eyes. "Lots of auditions for animated villains, but studios keep going for big names instead."

Voice acting was not something Audra had ever considered, and she had a million questions. But the conversation had already shifted, the other man launching into a story about when he "had" to play Gaston at the park last year.

In the weeks that followed, Audra had googled "Tess Monroe voice actor" innumerable times, though she hadn't yet found the courage to purchase one of her audiobooks. But even that seemed far easier than talking to Tess about it directly. There was so much she needed to learn, yet she was afraid of looking like a fool by asking something stupid.

The more she heard about Tess around rehearsals,

and then later at performances, the more she knew this woman was exactly who Audra aspired to be. Confident, talented, funny, and attractive, and successful, and a magnet for making new friends wherever she went. Offstage, she was charming, while at the same time, onstage, the effortless, stone-cold authoritarian her role required. It was Tess who decided where everyone would go after a Friday night rehearsal, and Tess who had been cast as Nurse Ratched (to everyone's delight).

And now, on this last night of the show, it was Tess who showed up first and who Audra could have the most time with. This was her last chance to make one of her cast members a real friend—someone who might invite her to come see them in *One Flew Over the Cuckoo's Nest*, for example. Each person in the cast had everyone else's phone number and email address from the cast list, but that didn't mean any of them would use it. Not for *Audra*.

The Atlas Theater held three dressing rooms for the women, and three dressing rooms for the men, just barely enough space for a cast this size. Audra realized that since she'd gotten there so early and set out the thank-you notes, Tess could not help but know that she was in the building too.

Would it be enough to bring her over? To seek Audra out?

The door to the alley opened again, and Audra heard the laughing chatter of several of the other cast members, and then the entire cast piled into backstage in groups of twos and threes over the next forty minutes. Audra kept getting interrupted as more people entered.

And the quiet moment she could have had with Tess was gone.

Soon her own dressing room was full of nearly a dozen women and girls, greeting one another, finding their chairs, starting their own hair and makeup, trading closing night gifts, hurriedly finishing their fast-food dinner, and downing their energy drinks. Audra got lost in the hubbub, trying to soak it all in this last time. The stage manager knocked briefly to remind them that the theater owner and her husband would be in the audience that night.

"Five minutes!"

"Thank you, five," Audra responded in chorus with the others, as she took the hot rollers out of her hair.

Five minutes was not nearly enough time to initiate what she hoped would be a memorable interaction. Though the first scene of the show would not require either Tess or her, she knew better than to distract any of her fellow actors after the curtain rose. As one of the few actors on that cusp between the kids of the cast and the adults, Audra took her professionalism very seriously. There would be no dismissing of her simply because she played one of the teenagers.

With that, the final five minutes rushed by, backstage lights dimmed, and the show began.

Audra's role was mostly ensemble, with a handful of highlighted moments, and as such it was perfect for her. She'd never aspired to stardom, and a role like this allowed her to be part of so much more of the production. Singing, dancing, a couple lines, a couple costume changes, and then . . .

Curtain call for the last time.

Audra held hands in a long row with the rest, smiling,

bowing, happy tears in her eyes as she let the sound of applause wash over her.

She would do anything to be part of something like this again as soon as she could.

But now was closing night, and here were her parents, come to see her last show, kissing her cheek and telling her to have fun. Audra had the whole night ahead of her, to fill as she chose, and this was exactly where she wanted to be: the cast party, the celebration that marked their collective accomplishment of another show ended.

The party itself was at the deceptively modest mid-century home of the woman—and her husband—who owned Atlas Theater. As it was just a mile or so away, most of the adults in the cast carpooled there, leaving their cars at the theater and freeing themselves for a night of revelry. Audra had found that, in most situations like this, if she was around and paying attention when rides were offered, she was always included. That was part of the community of theater, after all. She had packed her tote bag full of all the bits and notes and ephemera that had marked this production, and said her own silent goodbye to the theater before squishing into the backseat of a car with three other women just a bit older than her.

The dozens of cast members trickled into the house, eager for the flirting and alcohol and appetizers and stories and the long goodbyes. Once the interior of the house grew too warm with all the bodies, they began spilling out into the cold January night on the back patio. Audra made her own tentative efforts to join conversa-tions here and there, but found herself constantly distracted keeping track of where Tess Monroe was.

Could she maneuver her way to Tess's side without being too obvious about it?

When she was amusedly listening to one of the teenage boys trying to hit on her, she noticed Tess rise from her seat, a green, velvet chaise in the corner. She crossed in front of Audra, entering the kitchen. Audra turned away again, trying to at least be polite to the poor boy who was trying to compliment her, but she just could not find the energy to feign interest. There was no point in pretending otherwise; she murmured her excuses and followed Tess into the kitchen.

The light was far brighter than it had been in the living room, and it was smaller than she expected. Audra paused in the doorway, taking in the sight. Though the house was remodeled and luxuriously appointed, it was still a house built in the 1940s, with the narrow galley kitchen that came with post-war tract homes. Though she had planned to come grab a drink, the tight quarters meant that she could not possibly do so without getting inches away from Tess, who was now leaning into the open fridge.

"Oh!" Audra stopped short. "I—I came for a drink?"

"Hey," Tess said, looking up briefly before turning her focus back to the interior of the fridge. "I don't know what I'm looking for."

Audra grinned like an idiot at the older woman's brief attention, and had to turn away to keep from embarrassing herself too badly. She'd been reasonably sure that she would find Tess, as she always was, surrounded by friends and admirers. Finding her alone had thrown Audra off entirely.

"Anything, uh, good in there?" she asked, wincing inwardly.

She took a small step closer, hesitant to crowd her.

"Nah." Tess closed the fridge and moved to the other side of the small galley kitchen. "That's not a surprise when there's so many kids here."

She stepped past Audra, who briefly felt as though Tess's comment had been a pointed criticism. But then she stopped in the doorway and turned back to Audra with a mischievous look in her eye.

"This party sucks," she muttered, quietly enough that only Audra heard her. "Grab who you want and meet me on the street in ten minutes."

And then she was gone, out of the kitchen before Audra could respond. She watched Tess make surreptitious moves around the room, whispering something presumably similar to her friends, all the while giving the theater owner a wide berth.

She hesitated. In part because she didn't quite believe Tess had meant that invitation for *her*, but also because this was the closing night cast party. She had been looking forward to this for months. This cast party would never happen again.

But, then, neither would this invitation to hang out in a smaller group with Tess Monroe.

Audra was not one for impulses, but she would not let herself miss this chance.

It was just before midnight, and really there was no reason she couldn't reasonably leave now. There was no one she wanted to invite to join her and Tess, so after a moment, Audra grabbed her coat and her bag. Once those were in her hands, several of the other cast members noticed she was leaving and exclaimed over her, hugged her, wished her goodbye, made promises to keep in touch. It was all very sweet, but she knew it was just the special magic of cast parties, that all their intentions to keep in touch could and probably would be wiped away with the remnants of stage makeup. She was able to slip out without too much fanfare and soon was standing by the quiet suburban street late on a January night.

A couple people had preceded her, another couple behind her, and soon she stood with half a dozen other actors from the cast and crew, awkward on the sidewalk, looking up and down the street for their ringleader.

Just when Audra was afraid that she'd missed her chance, Tess came striding out of the front door.

"Who's got a car?" she called to the group. When no one immediately answered, she said, "Follow me."

Audra knew quite well she was just tagging along with older, cooler, more interesting, more adultier adults. But she figured if she stayed quiet and did not draw attention to how very young—how very *lame*—she was then no one would insist she leave. That was how she found herself squished in the backseat of Tess's Avalon, listening to the tenor sitting next to her belt the big solo from *Miss Saigon*.

Audra was grateful she wasn't driving. She didn't want to have to pay attention to anything as mundane as traffic laws when she could be letting the magic of that moment sweep over her. Gorgeous music. Irreplaceable company. She was certain she must be grinning like an idiot, but she couldn't care less; she literally could not remember the last time she'd been this happy. The only thing that could make this night better, she thought, was if she was in the front seat, hearing stories about how Tess got into voice acting.

As Audra had only been paying attention to the car's interior, she didn't realize until they were already parked that Tess had led her small caravan to a hole-in-the-wall bar, only half full despite it being a Saturday night. The sight of this reminded Audra that she was again the youngest of the group by several years. She was still three months shy of her twentieth birthday—was this the kind of place that would even let her in the door?

She needn't have worried, arriving as she was with Tess Monroe.

The group piled out of the car, ran across the four-lane city street, and poured through the front door. As soon as she'd stepped across the threshold, Tess called to the bartender.

"Ollie!"

Straggling in the back of the group, Audra didn't hear what was said between them, wasn't thinking about anything beyond the very real possibility that she could get kicked out and have to find a ride home past midnight. But after a few moments milling around the small, dark space, some of her fellow cast members had pulled together a couple tables in the middle of the room while others had collected a round of beers from Ollie.

Audra saw with no surprise that she'd ended up with an empty seat next to her. In all her efforts to be unobtrusive and not draw attention, she had somehow managed to stay completely invisible for the few months the company had been rehearsing and performing. Everyone else had their little alliances, their dalliances, and she sat with her hand around the neck of the cold

Miller High Life, listening to the snatches of conversation around her.

"You don't like beer?" a low voice said from behind her.

Audra startled as Tess took the empty chair to her left.

"What? No, I— Sorry, I—"

"Relax." Tess grinned and gestured to the bar. "Get something else if you want. Ollie will put it on our tab. They're one of my roommates. Honest, get whatever you want."

"Thanks, no, this is fine."

Audra hurriedly took too big of a gulp, the beer's tartness and slight carbonation surprising her into a light coughing fit.

"You all right there?" Tess asked, patting her on the back. "Didn't mean to startle you."

"No, sorry, I—" Audra cleared her throat, shaking her head a little bit. "I'm all right. Thanks."

"Sure."

And with that, Tess leaned forward, toward the woman across the table from her, asking some teasing question about the audition the woman had gone to earlier that week, and seeming to forget Audra altogether.

She took another sip of the beer, more deliberate this time. Choking to death was not how she wanted to get Tess's attention. She wished she'd had something witty to say before Tess's interest had moved on, but sitting next to her, close enough to pretend to be part of her conversations, was the next best thing.

Audra found herself crossing her legs just like Tess did, leaning forward on one elbow like Tess was, trying to anticipate what questions Tess would ask that made her so freaking charming to everyone else. If showing an interest in other people was what it took to be liked, Audra could learn to do that. Or, rather, she could learn to express the interest she already had. Tess seemed to be a master at getting whoever she was talking with to light up and love her for the opportunity.

All that said, though, Audra was still only just watching. Even though she was sitting in the middle of the table, at Tess's right elbow, she still felt rather left out of things. There was a conversation with everyone on the end of the table to her right, and another with everyone on the end of the table to her left, but here in the middle no one gave Audra a second glance. After another several minutes of trying and failing to act as though she belonged there, she got up and walked over to the bar.

Ollie looked up when they heard her coming, offering a broad, welcoming smile as she sat on the barstool in front of them. A deep dimple flashed in each cheek when they smiled. They had short, spiky, purple hair, a full sleeve of tattoos on their left arm, and a ring pierced into their lip. So, probably not an actor, Audra thought.

"You want another of those?" Ollie asked, indicating the half-full bottle in Audra's hand. "Or something else? Don't feel like you need to finish it if you hate it. It's fucking Miller, after all."

"No, I don't hate it, I just thought . . . I kinda felt like I was in the way over there. Wanted some, uh, air," she finished lamely, looking around and registering the fact that she was still indoors, in a tiny, full bar, four feet from another patron.

"Tess can become a black hole of attention," Ollie said wryly.

Audra's mouth fell open. What kind of friend—?

"I'm kidding," they said, placing their hand on her wrist. "Jesus, sorry. Bad joke. I have so many regulars here, I forget not everyone knows my sense of humor. No, sorry, it's a running joke in our apartment. Of the four of us, Tess is the only actor, *and* she works from home and is constantly on the rest of us to keep quiet. We joke about the world revolving around her, that the rest of us are just planets in her orbit. You get it."

"Yeah . . . that's funny."

"Of course, if anyone else said that about her I'd roast them in return until they cried, but so far that hasn't happened yet. Makes friends everywhere, doesn't she?"

"She seems cool."

Audra looked back over her shoulder at where Tess was regaling her half of the table with some story that involved her puffing up her chest and shoulders to look bigger.

"And not just because she got you a free drink, I'm guessing?"

Turning back to Ollie, Audra shrugged sheepishly. "I'm not really a drinker. I don't know if I like this beer or not, because I think it's the first time I've *had* beer. Like, ever."

A burst of laughter from the tables behind her startled Audra, though she reminded herself they could not possibly be laughing at her, couldn't possibly have heard her confession.

"Yeah?" Ollie said. "Well, let's see how else we can corrupt you."

They grabbed a clean pint glass from the counter and

filled it about two inches high with something pulled from one of the taps.

"Try this," they said, setting it in front of her. "It's heavier than what you've been drinking, much richer of a drink."

Audra sipped it cautiously, not wanting a repeat of the choking she'd endured when sitting next to Tess. The thick, malty beverage seemed to coat her mouth. It was a bit sweet, and she thought she might be imagining it, but there was something chocolatey about it too.

"That's *good*." She took another sip, and felt a warmness start to spread through her chest. "It is awfully rich, though, isn't it? Is it—is that Guinness?"

"Ah, so you're not a complete heathen."

"One of my uncles went to Ireland five years ago. He still talks about how it's the only place to drink Guinness."

Ollie laughed. "Okay, then. Don't tell him you had some in West Hollywood without even a proper head on it."

Audra blinked and looked around as Ollie busied themself behind the bar. As she had barely tasted alcohol before this night, she had no idea if what she was feeling was normal or not. It was possible she just was too petite, too hungry, or too tired to be able to handle more than a few sips.

She kind of wanted to try something else.

The warmth and lightheadedness was delightful, Audra thought, as she considered returning to the table with the others. Someone had scooted over and taken her seat next to Tess in the intervening time, though.

"All right, one more experiment."

Ollie set a shot glass in front of her. It wasn't quite full, but even that much was more hard alcohol than she'd ever had before. Half a glass of mimosa with her mom and aunts every occasional girls' weekend. And once, at a friend's graduation party, her dad had made a "signature," extremely watered-down cocktail. But it had far too much mint and sugary syrup in it, so Audra didn't even drink a whole glass.

This, under Ollie's guidance, would be a very different experience.

She picked it up, the clear liquid lulling her into underestimating it.

"You cannot sip it," Ollie clarified. "I can't let you do that. Just down the hatch. Come on. I know you've got it in you."

"What is it?"

"Grey Goose. Keep it in the freezer, and just dole it out a tiny bit at a time like this."

Audra nodded and grinned. To her surprise, she was enjoying herself. Though she'd hoped that this whole closing-night, cast-party, hanging-out-with-Tess thing would have gone differently, she couldn't complain about this cute, friendly bartender helping her broaden her experiences.

Just as she was about to throw her head back and swallow the mouthful, someone put a hand on her shoulder. She turned, hoping it was Tess, but was startled to see a strange guy standing there, practically looming over her. He wore a worn Lakers crewneck sweatshirt from the '90s and seemed old enough that Audra wondered if he had bought it new, instead of finding it in a thrift shop. In the dim light of the bar she couldn't be certain of the man's age, but she'd guess it was close to her dad's.

"Pretty girl like you shouldn't be drinking alone," he said, a tiny slur to his words.

"Oh lord," Ollie murmured, but Audra was pretty sure the man hadn't heard.

"I'm fine," she said tightly.

"No, no, you get me one of those and I'll have a shot with you."

She looked to Ollie uncertainty, and while the bartender gave her a meaningful look, Audra had so little experience in situations like this that she couldn't begin to interpret it.

"Um . . ." she said. "No, thank you."

Ollie snorted a soft laugh.

"No, really, it's no trouble. My friends don't even miss me." He gestured to a table against the far wall where two other guys about his age were sitting and watching him. Taking the barstool closest to Audra, he leaned even closer. Judging from his breath, he had likely been here for a few hours.

"I'm not buying drinks tonight," Audra said with a patient smile. Maybe that was all he wanted from her—a free drink.

The man shook his head, like a disappointed father. "I think she could use something a little stronger," he said to Ollie, while not taking his eyes off Audra.

Suddenly she wished she hadn't left Tess's side. Even if she hadn't exactly been participating in the conversation, at least she'd been insulated on all sides from interlopers like this.

"I think she's just fine," Ollie said. "Why don't you tell me your drink order? I'll add it to *your* tab, and then you can go back to your table."

He glanced over his shoulder again at his friends watching him, and then back to Ollie. "Nah, I think I'll drink this one here. Whatever she's having."

Ollie glanced at Audra, as though to check she'd be okay without them, before saying, "Coming up."

All the warmth and friendliness from the bartender was gone. And so was their comforting presence, leaving Audra alone with this drunk older man.

"It's just a shot," he said wheedlingly as he leaned closer to her. "We'll have a shot together, so you don't have to drink alone tonight."

"You know, I appreciate the offer," she said, lacing all the sarcasm she could muster into her tone, "but I'm not buying drinks for anyone tonight. Because I'm only nineteen. Legal, technically, to be annoyed by you, but not to buy you a drink."

As he spluttered his protests, Ollie set a shot glass in front of him.

"But if you want to drink with a teenage girl," Audra continued, "maybe check and see what your daughter is doing?"

"Bitch," he muttered, as he half fell off the stool and walked back to his table.

Ollie roared with laughter, and Audra was grateful for the low lighting, which hopefully hid her embarrassed blushing.

"What's so funny?" Tess asked, calling from where she sat at the table.

"Your girl Audra here put that joker in his place," Ollie reported, loud enough for the rest of the bar to hear.

"Oh yeah?"

Tess stood up and came to stand next to Audra at the bar, though her eyes were glued to the receding back of the man who had inserted himself into her friends' conversation. Ollie told the whole story, making Audra sound far cooler than she deserved. She quickly threw back the shot of vodka, before Ollie could take it back from her, and immediately decided that was plenty of alcohol for her either way.

"I'm going to pretend I didn't hear you say you're nineteen," Ollie whispered, quickly moving the half-full bottle of beer and empty pint and shot glass from in front of Audra. "And you're going to drink water or soda the rest of the night."

They were gone again before Audra could apologize, but somehow she hadn't felt as though she was being scolded.

Just as Tess reached the bar, Ollie sat a cocktail napkin and highball glass in front of Audra; the drink looked brown in this light.

"It's a dark 'n' stormy," they explained. "With my special twist on it."

Audra took a cautious sip, immediately recognizing that the special twist was likely in making the drink nonalcoholic. She was so grateful to her new friend for not only drawing attention to her age by kicking her out, but going so far as to help her disguise it.

"Come back to the table," Tess said. "We can't leave you here on your own to fend off *Lakers fans*."

"Thanks for the drinks," Audra said to Ollie.

"I'll see you again," they said. "Maybe not here though, huh?"

Audra smiled gratefully, taking her new drink and following Tess back to the table. When they got there, Tess made the woman who had slipped into Audra's seat move.

"Hey, you guys, our little Audra has a surprise streak of sass in her," Tess began, telling the story all over again and making Audra sound far more clever and cool than she'd ever been in her life.

In Tess's retelling, however, Audra began to believe that she *was* that clever. That she *was* that cool and collected. Seeing herself through someone else's eyes had the effect of instilling far more confidence in her than she thought possible.

But maybe that was just the magic of Tess Monroe.

The conversation soon turned from Audra's antics, but she didn't mind. Being the star of the show had never been her goal. Instead, she sat at Tess's side and was occasionally asked questions, deferred to, included in group jokes. The vodka had settled her nerves, she suspected, and she was again immensely happy with how her night had evolved.

The clock struck one in the morning, then one thirty. The rest of the cast left one or two at a time, but Audra couldn't make herself leave Tess's side. Until, finally, it was just Tess, Audra, Ollie, and a one of the barbershop quartet guys whose boyfriend had come to the show and cast party but then left when they broke for the bar. When he finally got up to leave, Tess did too.

"Ollie's about to yell at me." She began pulling the

tables apart again. "They are insistent that I work off at least some of what I drink when I come in here."

Audra stood to help straighten the tables and move the chairs back. "Let me help."

"Almost done. Nice of you to stay this long, though. I guess you're not working tomorrow?"

Audra shook her head, unwilling to admit out loud that her parents didn't want her to work at all while she was going to school. But tomorrow was Sunday, so no school. Or, rather, *today* was Sunday. She'd kept her phone at the bottom of her bag, but a glance at the clock on the wall over the bar told Audra that it was almost two in the morning.

"I'll see you at home," Tess called to Ollie.

The latter waved her off, as they stood over the table of guys in the corner, gesturing something about how they too needed to get going.

Tess and Audra stepped outside, the cold night air stinging their cheeks.

"You got a ride?"

"Oh, um. No? I can call a car though."

"You can't live that far. Get in." Tess pointed to her beat-up Toyota parked across the street and started to jaywalk before Audra could protest. "Besides," she said, unlocking the car, "it's not like I'm going to leave you here alone."

"Thank you," Audra gushed.

The car turned on, and Tess let it run a minute so the heat could warm up.

"Where are we going?" she asked, clicking in her seatbelt.

"You can just drop me off at the theater," Audra murmured.

"Oh yeah? You leave your car there?"

"Something like that."

They drove in silence for another block before Tess said bluntly, "What do you mean, 'something like that'? Tell me where your car is, and I'll take you there. Don't be silly."

"I—I don't have a car."

"Then, what? You *live* at the theater?"

Tess sounded exasperated; Audra couldn't let this be the last impression she had of her.

"I took an Uber," she muttered. "And I'll take an Uber home."

"Just tell me where home is, you ridiculous girl."

Tess flipped her turn signal, despite the fact that they hadn't seen more than two cars in the last ten minutes. This time of night most people were either home already, or out some place they didn't want to leave.

There were only a few blocks left until they reached the theater and Audra left Tess forever.

This was her last time, her last chance to make any kind of impression on this woman, and she wanted it to be a good one.

Audra thought about how in Tess's retelling she had seemed so together, so confident, and she had a vague idea that Tess would value honesty.

"I don't want you to see where I live," she blurted out. "I want you to keep whatever cool, interesting impression you have of me."

Tess looked at her sharply, then a smirk creeped across her face as she turned back to the road.

Another quiet moment, then: "You're, what? Nineteen, right?"

"Yeah."

"Oh god." Tess laughed again, that deep, throaty chuckle making Audra feel like she didn't mind being teased if it meant hearing that laugh. "All right, Nineteen. Whatever you say. Theater it is."

The final few blocks to the Atlas were silent. Audra almost wished there was some other musical playing through the car speakers, but more than anything she didn't want to leave Tess with a bad impression of her. She could make fun of those Lakers fans again or ask her some insightful question about . . . what? While she had long ago resigned herself to the likelihood that she would never see this woman again, she still wanted whatever memory kept to be flattering.

Tess pulled into the parking lot next to the theater and stopped with the car still running. She looked at Audra and raised her eyebrows in question. When Audra still didn't say anything, she put the car in park.

"What's your name again?" Tess asked softly.

"Audra."

"That's right. Audra. My memory for faces is shit. Please don't take offense. It's why I overcompensate with loudness. Distractions. Anyway. Audra." Tess turned in the driver seat to face her. "Audra. I'm going to give you another chance because Ollie seemed to really like you. There's something here." She gestured at Audra's general person, like she was casting a spell. "You don't have to tell me, but I'd love to know what all this is about. Deflecting? Is it fake politeness? I offered you something you clearly needed, but you turned it down. Why is that?"

"I didn't think you meant it," Audra said in a small voice.

"Jesus Christ. You think I would lie to you about something like that? I don't even know you. I mean . . . girl. No offense, but I don't care enough to be fake-nice to a near stranger."

"Yeah . . . I get it."

Audra looked down at her hands in her lap. She had felt so accepted, so included, after that incident with the drunk guy, but now it seemed like she'd blown it completely.

"Look. And, please, don't take this as patronizing."

Audra looked up at her again, seeing actual concern on Tess's face. All through the previous few months, if pressed, she would have guessed that Tess was putting on some sort of act. She was the "cool girl." The charming one. Tess valued honesty, but that didn't mean she told you *all* of the truth. And while she didn't let anyone get too close to her, that didn't matter because she made you feel amazing about yourself.

But now, for some reason, Audra suspected she was letting herself be real. That Tess saw this nineteen-year-old girl and recognized that a few honest words could make a difference in her life.

She swallowed hard, waiting breathlessly for whatever Tess would say.

"I'm glad you came out with us tonight," Tess said, "even if Ollie is going to make fun of me for months." She chuckled ruefully. "Every time I walk in there, they're going to ask me if everyone I brought is over twenty-one." She sighed, that smirk briefly coming back. "Anyway, I was nineteen once. I get it. Everything seems like a big deal. Life-and-death if this woman you barely know realizes that you live somewhere . . . I don't know. Not cool?"

Audra nodded, and Tess took a deep breath, softening her smile.

"Honey. You have no idea how lucky you are right now. You have so much time. Being perceived as 'cool' is not the priority you think it should be. Do you understand what I'm saying?"

"It's not that," Audra protested, suddenly distraught to think that Tess might leave thinking all she cared about was looking cool.

"What is it then?"

"I just . . . I want to do what you do," Audra said finally. "Doing voice work from home during the day, and then at night doing theater or going out to a bar where you're friends with the bartender, and . . . it just seems so glamorous. It's like—it's kind of my dream life. I just wanted to delude myself a little bit longer that I could even belong in your world."

"God. Glamorous?" Tess said under her breath. "You would not find it *glamorous* if you had to shut yourself inside your closet and stop recording every fifteen minutes because some wannabe model who lives across the court-yard is day drinking by the pool and has a laugh as piercing as Janice."

"Who?"

"Never mind. This is even better than what I thought. If you know what you want to do, *really* want to do with your life, spend your time worrying about that rather than trying to impress anyone who doesn't actually matter."

"But . . . it seems so overwhelming. Between what I

have and what you have? That's, like . . . the Grand Canyon."

"All right. Here. Give me your phone."

Too stunned to question it, Audra handed her unlocked phone to Tess, who immediately went to the texting app and opened a blank message.

"I'm giving you a resource," she said as she typed. "I can't remember the actual URL, but if you google this person, and maybe something like 'audiobook' or 'podcast' or whatever, you'll find it. It's a short, free course on recording and editing audio."

She handed the phone back to Audra, who saw that Tess had texted herself this information.

"That's where you start. Do it for free at first, for friends or yourself. Practice a lot. Get known as much as you can. Kindness. Hustle. Being an easy person to work with is most important, so if you can do that *and* have talent, soon people will be offering to hire you. You've got my phone number now too," Tess finished, pointing at the phone. "Just in case something . . . I don't know. Disney needs a new princess and you've got questions. But that's how you close that Grand Canyon."

"Thank you," Audra said in a whisper, clutching her phone tightly.

"But believe me. Audra. You can do this. Plus, you're only nineteen! You have so much time and opportunity. Especially since you live with your parents, right?" she finished gently. "Having that kind of financial and emotional support is not something you should just discard because it's not cool or whatever."

"Okay, yeah. Yeah."

"Do you believe me?"

"Um . . ." Audra grinned in spite of herself. "I'm trying."

Tess laughed. "Close enough. Now, girl, stop being so damned coy and just tell me where you live, so I can drop you off and then finally go to bed. Some of us have big, glamorous days of auditioning for dog food commercials tomorrow."

———————————

The First Time It Happens

———————————

The first time it happens is several years into their relationship. There have been fights and disagreements, but never before has he raised his voice. Especially not like this, loud enough for the neighbors to hear.

She has never been yelled at before. Not like that. Not sharp enough and loud enough to make the cat run and hide.

She has never been yelled at before.

Never.

Not by her father. Not by her ex-husband. Not by a boss or during a breakup.

(Strange that it doesn't occur to her that any woman in her life would shout at her.)

She looks at him blankly. Feels disconnected from the entire situation.

What is the next step? How is she supposed to react to this?

When she says, "That is not appropriate," he yells

louder, telling her he doesn't give a fuck what is appropriate.

Being the calm one doesn't seem to help.

She sits, stunned, numb, unable to react, unable to even hear his angry words.

After a few minutes of venting, he falls silent.

"No one has ever yelled at me like that before," she says softly.

There is a pause. She can't look at him. She's afraid of what she'll see.

"Oh my god, I'm sorry."

She looks at him.

"I'm sorry," he says again, tears in his eyes. "I'm sorry. I'm so sorry. Baby, I'm so sorry."

He reaches for her. Grabs for her. Holds tight to her, burying his face in her shoulder.

"I'm sorry I'm sorry I'm sorry. Oh my god, I'm so sorry."

She is numb, as though watching from outside herself.

This is what Instagram therapists would label a "red flag," isn't it?

"It's okay," she says automatically.

"I'm so sorry."

She rubs his back, round and round in circles.

"I know. Thank you. I know. It's okay."

———

THE SECOND TIME it happens is a few months later, and he doesn't yell. Not exactly. He's learned to control the volume of his voice. Mostly.

But there's still venom. There's still cursing. Still mocking and belittling in the way he speaks to her.

When she tries to point out the cruel way he is speaking, he gets angrier.

He accuses her of deflecting.

"Only people who don't have strong arguments twist it around and try to make it about the other person's tone," he says.

"I don't think I have a strong argument," she insists. "I was just trying to have a conversation."

———

THE THIRD TIME IT HAPPENS, she doesn't know what to do. He is still not as piercingly loud, but he is so angry he doesn't seem to care what words come out of his mouth. He doesn't seem to hear her. She doesn't understand how it escalated so quickly.

She panics. Her heart pounds.

She hyperventilates.

She can't feel her hands.

She tells him in a shaking voice, between rapid, shallow breaths, that she is afraid when he gets mad like that.

She gets up in the middle of the conversation and walks away, sitting on the floor of the kitchen for a few minutes while she catches her breath. She doesn't know what he's doing as she calms her heart.

When she returns, he says, ashamed, softly, "You really are afraid of me, aren't you?"

———

THE FOURTH TIME it happens she tries to yell back, tries to not be afraid. Maybe the only way he can hear her is if she stands up to him.

But she doesn't have the same anger that he does, the same loss of control, the same intent to wound.

And as if he senses that opening, he doubles down on his anger.

"Fuck off," he says again. "Fuck *off*."

———

THE FIFTH TIME IT HAPPENS, she asks again for him to stop cursing at her.

"I need to have an outlet," he insists. "I need to be able to express myself when this is *fucking* stupid. But"— he cools down almost imperceptibly, generously allowing her a point—"if you want to make it a rule that I can't curse *at* you, that I can't say 'fuck off'—"

"It's a rule," she says, expression cold.

———

THE LAST TIME it happens he is already so angry before the fight has even started that she is shocked by his ire, by the depth of his hate.

"Fuck off!" he yells as he strides off down the hall, away from her. "Fuck off! We're *done*."

And it's with that phrase that she finally feels relief.

Geese

White snow, harshly bright against the black pavement. Unblemished on the verge between the retail parking lot and the road. Against this backdrop of grays and blacks and whites, the birds' neutrals barely make an impression. Only movement reveals their presence.

Why have they not flown south?

What are they waiting for, hovering nearby?

<hr>

Just Below the Surface

<hr>

Last week, when I was having coffee with Cheryl and Sandy, the former told us about her son's recent car accident and hospital stay.

I got so angry I dropped my latte on the floor.

The paper cup, two-thirds full and still piping hot, just slipped from my grasp, hit the spotless tiled floor, and splattered everywhere. I cursed under my breath and got up immediately. One of the baristas, seeing the spill, brought over a roll of rough, brown paper towels, which I accepted before shooing her away. It was my mess; I would deal with it like I always do.

"I mean, the truck just blew through the stop sign," Cheryl was saying as I knelt down under the table. The coffee had almost splashed her shoes and she'd moved them away almost unconsciously. "If it had been going any faster, Joey would probably be dead right now."

"Oh my god," Sandy said, breathless. "You poor thing. It's so scary. When my sister got hit by a car, she had to spend a few days in the hospital. I ended up taking off a whole week of work, but I was just so thankful it wasn't worse."

"I remember that!" Cheryl said. "Didn't she lose all her hair or something?"

"Yes! With all the skull surgeries they had to do," Sandy said, "her husband just ended up having her head shaved. It grew in thicker after that, as a matter of fact."

As I knelt there, swiping up the last streaks of my coffee, listening to these inane details about people who aren't even smart enough to look both ways at an intersection, I wondered how on earth people end up in situations like that. This wasn't the first time I had just stood idly by while other people got all the sympathy and attention simply because they made a poor choice. It infuriates me. I work so hard to do everything right, and as a reward I get ignored.

I had been hoping to spend this little coffee klatsch to tell them that I finished my dissertation. I've been working on my PhD in cultural studies while also working full-time for more than seven years and I'm now so close to graduating. But I suppose that critical examination of the depictions of power in American political television shows isn't as interesting as almost dying in a car crash.

Being responsible and steady and mature is never as interesting as the alternative.

My childhood best friend almost drowned at her own birthday party. My cousin fell while zip-lining, shattering both of his legs. My other cousin *also* almost drowned. Two different friends from high school were in car accidents within the same year, one of them flipping their car at least four times. All the emergency personnel kept saying he should not have been able to walk away from that crash. Even my first ex-husband almost died from alcohol poisoning. Whenever it comes up in conversation now, everyone fawns over him, fascinated by his stupidity, asking questions about what it was like to wake up in a hospital when he was fourteen.

And here I am, calmly, safely, making the most practical choices, and no one cares. No one praises my level-headedness or my foresight. My caution gets me absolutely nothing but another unappreciated day.

Everyone I know has had a near-death experience except me.

It's not fair.

I deserve that same sympathy and curiosity. My life is just as interesting as theirs—more so, since I'm not an idiot.

I was glad my head was down, as I finished cleaning up the spilled latte. Cheryl took her time exhausting all the details about her son's car accident, but by the time she finally finished I had come up with my own plan.

I am going to make one of those inane choices—or appear to, at least. I'm going to put myself in one of those situations where things can go wrong if you let them, so the next time I'm at coffee or a party, I'll have my own story. It shouldn't be too difficult. Plenty of dummies do it all the time. I just need to make a couple different choices at exactly the right moments, and I'll have Sandy's envy and admiration at next year's holiday party.

Idiots don't get a monopoly on exciting stories. Not while I can still plan for one.

Why didn't I think of this before? Decades ago!

I've decided my own near-death experience will

happen on my fiftieth birthday. There's a lovely symbolism there, I think. And I have already started rehearsing how I will tell the story. No more playing it safe, no more being sensible and hardworking. No more missing out on the gasps of disbelief. However I have been living my life is not conducive to such dangerous adventure, so I'm making a specific effort to put myself in such a circumstance.

Happy half a century of boring sense to me.

———

I CHARTER a boat to take me out, off the coast of Long Beach, partway to Catalina. It's a small ship, just a captain and two crew members, all men, all of whom speak English as their second language. I didn't plan for that, but I imagine even this small language barrier will help make my story even more riveting. We leave midafternoon and sail leisurely toward the island until sunset, when we anchor for an hour or so. I've packed what are essentially props for my cover story: a picnic lunch, bottle of wine, and journal.

Once we have anchored, I ostentatiously down a whole glass of rosé, all the while trying to appear as distraught as possible. I tell the captain I'm marking the anniversary of my husband's death and I wish to be alone. He purses his lips, but nods his agreement and herds his crew all the way to the bow—the one place from which they cannot see me.

I sit at the stern and lower my feet off the boat's edge into the water. It's colder than I expected for June, and goosebumps prickle all over my skin. The low waves lap against my legs and the side of the boat, splashing up as high as my knees.

I have this all planned out. I've known how to swim since I was a child, so all I need to do is shut down that instinct just long enough to be dramatic.

I take a deep breath and drop down feetfirst into the Pacific Ocean.

With my legs straight, knifing into the drink, I sink quickly, almost below the boat. Feeling its massive body block the sunlight panics me for a moment, before I remember what I'm doing and why. Slowly, I let out the air in my lungs and kick toward the surface farther out, away from the boat. I don't want to be close enough that the crew can easily see me, let alone easily pull me out. This is not going to work unless I'm fully on my own for several minutes.

I've just about run out of breath in my lungs. I need to make sure I'm the right distance away from the surface.

I force my eyes open. The salt stings, but not as much as the fire in my lungs.

I'm deeper than I expected to be—I must have swum lower than I intended. My best estimate puts the surface at least fifteen feet above my head. Nearly three times my height.

My legs are getting tired already.

My head is pounding, but I know it's too early to let up. I feel my pulse in every inch of my body, my heart desperate to keep my body going.

Even though I was sure I had let out all my air, I seem to find another reserve, my diaphragm forcing out every molecule.

That survival instinct is kicking in. I knew it would. I

make a compromise with my lizard brain and kick up a little closer to the surface. Still maybe ten feet to go before I can take a breath again.

I'm close.

I'm so close . . .

I wonder if maybe I've done enough. If I reach the surface now, will the crew be worried enough to back up my claim of "near death"?

But I hate to do a thing halfway, so I count to five before kicking up to the surface again. The longer I can stay down here the better; the more dramatic the tale, the more sympathy and exciting twists and turns when I get to tell the story.

I keep thinking, *Another few seconds.*

Just another couple seconds . . .

But each second feels like a minute.

I look up toward the light, toward the air. My eyes burn.

My heart beats faster. The panic returns, climbs.

I feel like my head might explode. I need air. I need oxygen.

I need to give it up. I need to trust I've been down here long enough. I need to use the little energy I still have to save myself. I may be trying to be an idiot, but I should at least be smart about it.

I kick, I paddle my arms. I use all the energy I have to try to get to the surface.

I don't know how much longer I can resist the instinct to take a breath.

I have to get to air.

I don't seem to be making any progress.

I've almost lost track of which way is up.

I lift my head toward the surface—I think that's the surface, yes, the light, the sun—focused intently on the air that is just there, just a few feet away. I just need to get there and I can take the breath I so desperately want.

I purse my lips closed as I desperately struggle upward.

I don't know how long I can do this.

I'm seeing spots in my vision. The lack of oxygen is having its effect.

I am too deep. I'm just below the surface, but even those three feet are too many.

I can't stop myself. I can't restrain my instincts any longer. I open my mouth for air, even as I know I'm still too far below the surface.

Water pours into my mouth, into my lungs.

I cough, or try to, to expel it, but instead only suck in more water.

I try to scream.

No one can hear me.

Water is getting into my lungs, but coughing more won't help.

Oh, no.

What have I done?

I need to fix this. I need to clean up this mess.

But I've made the wrong choice.

The pressure on my torso is unrelenting. I half-heartedly kick, trying to make my way back to the surface, but the lack of oxygen has shut down my muscles. I keep thinking some latent survival instinct will kick in any second, the power I've been holding back will somehow appear.

But I'm too tired. Whatever last burst of adrenaline I am counting on must have come and gone already.

I look up toward the surface, where the warm sunset light filters in through the water.

Six feet down.

Ten feet down.

Twenty.

Without the motion of my legs propelling me, without the air in my lungs giving me buoyancy, I sink lower and lower.

My last thought before I black out is wondering how Cheryl will tell this story the next time she's out to coffee. It's not fair that she'll get all the attention, but I wish I could be there to see it.

Converse

"Fuck it!" Bonnie said out loud to her empty apartment. "There's got to be something here . . . *Something.*"

From her weird squat, she leaned forward and dug through the bottom of her coat closet, through years' worth of shoes and gift wrap and orphaned gloves and cleaning implements and possibly-broken umbrellas and a half-full box of nails and Lord knew what else. She couldn't even remember the last time she'd looked below the row of hanging coats. There used to be an intact pair of Converse in here, she thought. That wasn't the best choice, but it would be better than the Keds, wouldn't it? It was something.

She sneezed. Dust bunnies floated through the closed-in space.

Her knuckles hit something hard, nicking a little cut on the corner of something she couldn't see. Bonnie winced, making a mental note to clean this closet out sometime. Not now, though. If she paused even briefly and lost her momentum, she'd never make this change.

And something needed to change.

At this point she wasn't sure it mattered what. Just . . . *something*.

She had not paid attention to anything outside of her bare minimum of survival in . . . Bonnie paused to count.

Five years.

Five years of work and work and work and eating just enough calories to keep going so she could work some more and turning off her brain when she couldn't focus on work.

When she'd moved in five years ago, this apartment was supposed to be a place where she and her then-boyfriend lived together, but when he'd broken up with her because he felt "emasculated" (read: she got a new job and suddenly made more money than him), Bonnie had moved here on her own. At first that choice had been to spite him, to prove she didn't need him to build the life of her dreams, to further show off the fact that she was financially independent without a man. But then COVID happened and the world shut down and it would not have been safe for her to try to move. And then, because the world shut down and people weren't building commercial properties like they had before, her job security melted away. No one was buying window treatments for big offices, and Bonnie was lucky if she could even book a sales call, let alone close a deal. She wasn't risk tolerant enough to try to take on the expense of moving. And then —again, because of COVID—less new construction meant rent went up all throughout her city, and she wouldn't have been able to afford living somewhere else unless she had three roommates, and by then she was thirty-three years old and the idea of sharing a bathroom with a stranger made her even more depressed than the idea of saving money by eating ramen.

And thus, five years had gone by without her noticing. The dream life she'd thought she was creating for herself had become just day after day of working at a job she merely tolerated to keep a roof over her head and food in her fridge, neither of which she particularly liked.

One tiny choice after another tiny choice after another tiny choice had brought her to this place that she didn't recognize.

"Ah!" she murmured, as her fingers got tangled in the dirty, fraying shoelaces she'd been looking for. Both of the deep purple Converse low-tops—bought as part of her bridesmaid outfit for her older sister's wedding—were together, and as Bonnie pulled them out of the closet and sat back on her heels in the hallway, she brushed off the dust and hair and tiny scraps of paper—where had those come from?—and examined them. No cracks in the rubber soles. No knots in the laces. Not exactly the best choice but, again, it was *something*.

She had just gotten home from work after forty-five minutes in her car in Los Angeles traffic—relatively quick for this time of day. The drive, however, had been almost entirely on autopilot, because her thoughts were so full of what she'd overheard at work that afternoon.

Bonnie had arrived at her cubicle to find an email from HR letting her know that if she didn't use a week's worth of paid time off by the end of the calendar year, she would lose it. With a sigh, wishing that her company was one that would pay out that time instead of snatching it away, she looked at her calendar half-heartedly. She didn't have any plans, had no extra money, and couldn't think of a single reason to take five whole days off, but she might as well do something with it rather than lose it completely.

As she thumbed through the wall calendar that hung in her cubicle, wondering if the days on either side of any holidays were already unavailable, she heard the contagious, belly laugh of one of her coworkers.

"No, no, watch again," Shari said, before breaking up into laughter again. "She's so intent on the *drama* of it, she doesn't really notice that she's not doing a proper cartwheel!"

Bonnie peeked over the top of the cubicle wall to see Shari and Lisa, both moms of elementary-age kids, tight together watching a video on Shari's phone. The sound from the video was tinny and small from those little speakers, but to Bonnie it sounded like some dramatic power ballad that kids make up choreography to in their bedrooms. Bon Jovi? Maybe Bryan Adams?

"She has just been so enamored with the Olympics, oh my god, I can't even tell you. She did the same thing four years ago, but of course she doesn't remember."

"Oh my god, it's precious," Lisa agreed. "Will you put her in gymnastics now?"

Shari laughed again. "She has not stopped asking since the opening ceremony last week. She's already talked me into buying a yoga mat just so she can start practicing."

Bonnie sank back down into her office chair, careful to not let the women know she'd been eavesdropping.

If smartphones had existed in her childhood, there

would certainly have been videos of Bonnie and her sister doing much of the same things that Shari had captured her own daughter doing. Her sister, Ava, was four years older—a big enough gap to make her very bossy, insisting she was in charge, but a small enough gap that she still wanted Bonnie for a playmate.

She missed Ava. Bonnie hadn't seen her sister since the wedding four years ago, just before she moved all the way across the country for her new husband's job.

As Shari and Lisa watched the video again, Bonnie tried to remember what she and Ava had called themselves. The Strong Sisters? Something like that. Every two years, when the Olympics came around, their mom had made the whole couple of weeks a special event. They had Olympics-themed meals on the weekends, and their mom always made sure the collection of patriotic Old Navy T-shirts was clean.

But more than that, the Olympics was a time for Ava and Bonnie to level up their pretending. Synchronized swimming inspired them to synchronize their bike riding around the cul-de-sac. The balance beam had Bonnie walking carefully along the curb instead of the sidewalk for weeks. There was at least one day that she missed school at eight years old because her mother wouldn't let her attend in just a leotard and would rather call the office with an excuse than fight about it.

But the best for her and her sister was always the track and field events. Ava had an orange plastic stopwatch she got with five hundred arcade tickets one summer, and she would time Bonnie doing literally anything they could think of. How fast could she run to the stop sign at the end of the block and back? How fast could she run around the minivan ten times? How fast could she climb the tree in the backyard?

More of Shari's peals of laughter cut into her memories, and suddenly, Bonnie realized that she was . . .

She was *sad*.

It had been so long since she'd paid any attention to her emotions at all, and today, remembering what fun she used to have with Ava, what fun she used to have playing outside, running as fast as she could, pretending she was a world-class athlete . . .

Where had that all gone?

One tiny choice after another tiny choice after another tiny choice and then she was sitting in her cubicle, trying to force herself to use her paid time off—not for a vacation or anything fun, but to motivate herself to make some cold calls to office managers.

This could not continue.

Something needed to change.

Bonnie was so distracted the rest of the day that she made up an excuse to leave a little bit early, came straight home, her mind whirring all the while, and now was pulling on these barely worn purple Converse that made her miss her sister even more. Her entire drive home she didn't even listen to music; she was too busy thinking about all the fun and freedom and escape she used to have in her life that somehow, over the years, she'd lost.

She needed to do something about that.

The first thing that came to mind—easy, cheap, no real preparation required—was moving her body. Which was how she found herself on her knees, head deep in the bottom of the coat closet, looking for passable tennis shoes.

Something had to change or nothing would ever change and five more years would go by while Bonnie continued to just go through the motions of life, getting further into credit card debt because the only joy she allowed herself was whatever dopamine hit she got from buying something online that she hadn't really needed and would soon forget she owned while it collected dust in this closet.

How else had the coat closet become so full?

Still sitting in the middle of the hallway, Bonnie pulled on the purple Converse. She felt a bit manic, pushing herself to move, to get out of her rut, to make new choices before she lost the momentum. She retied the laces and stood, feeling the way the worn canvas fit around her feet. Standing up on her toes and then flattening her feet again, Bonnie felt something inside her shift.

She bounced on her toes a few times, a smile creeping across her face.

This was a familiar sensation, her feet in casual tennis shoes. It may have been years since she'd worn these shoes, but in the years before that it had been a daily occurrence. This was a part of her she'd not just let go of, but had forgotten about entirely. Though she was still wearing her business-casual-from-Target work clothes, her feet recognized this past version of Bonnie.

Two steps into her bedroom, where she found a sports bra at the bottom of a drawer and a pair of leggings on top of the dirty clothes pile. Quick quick *quick*, before she sat down again. Before she could talk herself out of it. She found a hair tie on the bedside table and threw up a ponytail, hair out of her eyes and off her neck.

Back down the hallway, and Bonnie had to pause at the front door. Phone? Ear buds? Keys? How did people do this? She had a vague memory of some app that helped you train for a marathon, but she didn't need that, did she?

The table just inside the entry had a shallow drawer, inside which Bonnie kept her spare set of keys. She dropped them in her cleavage, wincing slightly at the cold metal teeth. Looking around her apartment again, she tried to remember if there was anything else she should worry about.

She had not felt this interested in physical movement in . . . well, possibly ever. But something about the Olympics and the purple shoes and the stirring up the detritus of the closet made Bonnie feel like she could run for miles and miles.

Made her feel unaccountably proud of herself. Inertia could have run the rest of her life.

But even just this little bit was something.

Just before she stepped outside, Bonnie had one more thought. A quick google told her that the games would still be running another eight days, all day every day.

Before she left, she typed out a quick email to her boss: *Since I need to use that PTO, I'd like to take off the rest of this week. Call me if it's a problem, otherwise I'll see you Monday.*

With that, she set the phone—face down—on the little entryway table and opened her apartment door. August in Los Angeles was gross, and she already knew she'd be pouring sweat in about five minutes, but even that was enough of a novelty as to feel somewhat exciting.

Closing her apartment door behind her, Bonnie jogged down the steps to street level and began her tentative, exhilarating, unfamiliar run through her neighborhood, already thinking about talking to her sister about it when she got home. Maybe with a photo of her purple, distinctly-not-running shoes.

Maybe they could watch some Olympics together over the phone.

Your Exit

You look into your wine glass: just a mouthful of Syrah left at the bottom.

"Refill?" he asks, catching this. "I'm going to the bar."

You shake your head. "No, thanks." You swallow down the last bit, tipping your head back. "I think I'm going to call it a night."

The kind man with the reddish beard who you've been talking to for close to an hour nods, understanding. He opens his arms for a hug. "It was lovely talking with you. I'll definitely check out that book."

You step into his arms, talking to him with your chin on his shoulder. His hands on your back. For the short moment you are this close to another person, you feel safe. "And maybe I'll catch you at the signing next month? There's still tickets left, I think."

"Absolutely."

You step back, smile your gratitude, and turn to find a passing waiter with a mostly empty tray. You catch her eye, and she takes your empty glass from you before continuing on. With your back turned to the lovely, polite accountant who must be a former coworker of the host, you nudge your way through the crowd of guests.

You hadn't particularly wanted to come to this party tonight, but the host—the man who, short-limbed and at least fifteen years older than you, always puts his yoga mat next to yours at the Tuesday night classes—messaged you every day this week and three times just this morning about it; you had run out of excuses. Or maybe he just wore you down. Besides, what harm could there be? Your best friend, who you only see once a year anyway since she moved to Phoenix, keeps after you to make an effort. To not let your love of solitude keep you from the benefit of having actual, face-to-face friends in the city where you live, instead of just avatars on your phone.

"I'm going to a book signing," you insisted to her. "I work in an office with four other people. I go to yoga every week."

"You go to yoga because people are less likely to talk to you there," she returned.

"Why don't any of these studios offer *silent* yoga?" you joked.

But she's not wrong. Days—weeks, sometimes—will go by before you realize you haven't done anything beyond go to work and get groceries. And it will remain that way if you don't make a specific effort. If you don't pre-pay for the yoga classes as a hedge against canceling on yourself.

And so, when you finally agreed to come to this party hosted by the short, older man from your yoga class, the first thing you did was text your best friend.

Please clap, you said. *I made plans and there will be actual people there.*

But then, earlier this evening when you actually walked into the party, you remembered immediately why you don't like doing this. So many people. So much small talk. Squeezing yourself down to a surface-level, palatable version of yourself. Innocuous, unmemorable, unlikely to make any impression whatsoever. You told yourself you would stay long enough to have something to tell your best friend and then go home.

And now, you weave through the crowd—there must be close to a hundred people in this little three-bedroom suburban house—and spot the front door over the heads of the tallest.

Your host steps directly into your path. "Where are you going?"

"Home," you say. "Lovely party. Thanks so much."

But when you try to squeeze past him, he blocks the way, surprisingly effectively for how small he actually is. Shorter than you, but wide, feet planted heavily under him.

"You can't leave yet," he says. "You haven't even had a drink with me."

"I've had plenty to drink," you say with a polite smile. "Flattering, really, but I need to go. Work in the morning and all."

"Didn't you say you're on a summer schedule and go in midmorning every day?"

You freeze. You are almost certain you have never said anything about that to him. But he's not wrong. And it doesn't seem like the kind of thing he could guess, so you must have. Maybe in passing at the end of a yoga class.

Maybe you said it to someone else and he happened to overhear, and now has no shame about acknowledging the fact of his eavesdropping.

"Right. Midmorning. That's what I meant. I want to get lots of sleep tonight. There's just so much going on."

When you try again to move past him, there is simply no room at all. You look around, as though the clusters of conversations surrounding you are all in on the conspiracy to keep you locked in place. Will you have to physically move someone in order to make a path?

"Tell me." He grins at her, and it's almost predatory. "How'd you manage that schedule? Show a little leg and get a favor from the big boss?"

You furrow your brow. "No, my office does this every summer. It's just one of the perks."

"Oh." He nods. "Yeah. Yeah, my company has some pretty cool perks too. Hey, maybe you should come work with us. You could really rise through the ranks, I bet. I'm sure I could put in a good word. Maybe you and me meet up this week and talk over what kind of position you're looking for."

"I'm . . ." You don't even know where to start with your objections. "I'm not looking for another position. I'm quite happy where I am."

"Oh, come on. They can't pay you enough there. Not what you deserve. Do you really never think about what else is out there? Find someone who would really appreciate you?"

"I, um . . ."

You look over his shoulder at the door. It's so close. Maybe if you just go, just insinuate yourself forward, he'll get the hint. You smile tightly at him—standing this close, you have to actually look down a little—and move into the narrow space between his left shoulder and the woman standing with her back to him. He turns his body toward yours. You feel the warmth of his barrel chest on your upper left arm. You clench your left hand and bring it up in front of you, wary of accidentally touching anything you definitely do not want to touch.

"If you want, I can pass on your résumé," he says. "I don't think you have my email address, do you? Let me give you that."

He follows right behind you, close enough that even when you squeeze between two women on your way toward the door, they don't have a chance to block his progress.

You feel his hand on your upper arm.

"Give me your phone," he says. "I'll give you my contact."

"Oh, I can do it," you say, opening the Notes app that you barely use and will promptly forget about.

There are still at least half a dozen people between you and the front door. It occurs to you that if you leave the party now, he will likely follow you outside. And there are fewer people outside. Which feels even less safe than staying in his presence here in his house. At least here you're in a crowd.

You realize that you will not be able to get away until he finds something—someone—else to pour his attention over. You look around, only half-listening to him blather on about the NFTs he and his buddy are talking about "minting." Not six feet away is a woman you only know by sight, but enough to angle for an introduction. She looks to be exactly his type too.

But you realize before you take another step that you can't just transfer the creep to a different victim. You can't put another woman in an annoying situation (annoying at best; at worst, something far different).

You need to find someone who would not be this man's victim to palm him off on. Someone who would have no problem being rude to him if necessary. Who is not going to be worried about their physical safety. You read a book once about domestic violence and stalkers and how the seemingly nicest people could easily start obsessing to a dangerous degree. It's all you think about when you meet strange men now. He'd found you on Instagram and started messaging you there; it had taken months of yoga classes with him for you to even cave and respond.

"Right?" he asks, leaning into your face.

"Right," you agree with a tight smile, though you know you probably wouldn't actually agree with anything he could be saying. And shouldn't.

"Great." He beams at you. "Come with me."

When he turns away, you think maybe this is your chance. You take in a sharp breath, anticipating darting away through the crowd, but before he even takes a step he has turned around and grabbed your wrist.

"Don't want to lose you," he says with a wink.

"Wait—"

But he ignores you. When you try to withdraw your wrist, he squeezes more tightly without giving you a glance.

"Stop," you say.

But no one is giving you a glance.

"I don't want . . ."

But you trail off, noticing the way people in the crowd turn away from you. You could pull away more forcefully. You could make a scene. You could raise your voice and draw attention to the fact that he touched you without permission.

But how many people would come to your aid? How many people would step back and just watch? How many people would assume you're drunk or overreacting? This is his house. You came here voluntarily. You must have given him some kind of indication you were interested.

You did say "right," after all.

And so you follow, allowing yourself to be pulled back through the crowd, back through where you thought you had escaped, simply because you're not quick-thinking enough to come up with a safe alternative. Other people's gazes fall on you before slipping past, frictionless. No one seems to notice your alarm. No one is sparing you a second thought.

You should never have come here alone.

He is pulling you toward a door near the kitchen; you guess it leads to the garage or something similar. A dead end, where you will have no other escape and no one will overhear. You can't let him get you in there; you can't let him corner you. Sure, he *might* be relatively harmless, but it's safer to assume otherwise.

No one forcibly moving another person is completely harmless.

You drag your feet, purposefully extending the space between you and him, trying to allow for someone to get between you.

He tugs harder on your wrist, urging you closer.

You can't wait for someone else to rescue you.

You have to *do* something.

You plant your feet, resisting the pull on your left arm, while flailing out with your right arm. You make contact. A waiter passing with a tray of mini quiches tries to dodge, but your hand comes down on the edge of the tray, leveraging the quiches into the air. Several hit nearby guests. All bounce to the floor, where some are crushed underfoot. Smashed egg and pie crust stick to the faux wood, pieces clinging to the soles of shoes.

It happens so quickly that the guy manages to drag you another couple steps before he has noticed the mess and chaos.

He turns back at the noise.

"What—?"

"I'm sorry," you stammer, finally pulling your wrist free. "It's my fault. I lost my balance and—"

You crouch down, squatting to pick up the crumbly quiche with your bare hands. You avoid his eyes, trying to make yourself seem more pathetic, more in need of protection.

"Are you all right?" a nearby woman asks. She holds your elbow, keeping you steady as she helps you to stand before turning to the waiter. "Can we get some napkins?"

You flash her a grateful smile, using the commotion to take one small step farther from your host.

"Can't take you anywhere, huh?" your host mocks, looking down at the mess you have made. He wears a smile, but his eyes are cold. He looks around, noticing how much attention you have drawn to yourself. You see the moment his expression changes, when he decides you're not worth whatever small effort he might have otherwise made. When he dismisses you like the anonymous help he won't give a second thought to.

You back up another step, but he's already looked away from you.

"Clean this up," he says as he turns, so confident that his order will be obeyed that he doesn't bother addressing an individual.

You back up another step, almost disbelieving you might be successful.

"Napkins, ma'am," the waiter murmurs, as he hands you a small stack.

You keep watching your host until he has disappeared into the crowd. You're certain it will be only moments before he finds another unwilling listener or yes-man. You hurriedly wipe the smashed egg from your fingers, crumpling the soiled napkin in your fist.

The woman who helped you up is still watching you with concern.

"I'm fine," you say, backing up another step. "I'm just going to go wash my hands."

She nods, before turning to a friend.

You take another step away from the disaster, toward the front of the house. You are afraid to turn your back, but soon you are dodging your way through the crowd, as fast as you can. On your way out the door, you've already opened your phone to start searching for a new yoga studio.

First Step

First step: empty the joint bank account.

No, wait. First step should be to block Molly's phone number.

Oh, but, then she'll get really mad, and . . .

First step should be to stop sharing my phone location.

But, then, she checks on me randomly. She'll want to make sure I'm home before she comes back and will notice right away if I'm not, or if my location was turned off, and her temper will—

Okay, first step actually needs to be to call my cousin. Tori is the one person from whom Molly hasn't isolated me—we both know it's because she can manipulate Tori into buying us groceries or gas and things, but I'll take what I can get. Since my cousin moved closer to us, Tori has seen more of Molly's darkness than anyone else has. She's the one who helped me see the real disrespect in the way my wife talks to me, and she's heard me wonder how much longer I can take this. Everyone else in my life is effectively on Molly's side; Tori is the only person who might actually believe me that I am done for real this time.

I hope.

God, I hope she believes me.

Molly may only be with her mother for another hour or two. I need to go now while I can.

By now my boss has probably figured out that I'm not coming back to the office today, and I should use every single moment alone I have. It's going to be a whole thing tomorrow, but maybe I can convince him this was really the last time she's going to be a problem.

I hope that's true.

I have never in my life wanted more to be free of a person.

But I can't go without a car. And I can't call an Uber without the app sending Molly a notification. We're too deep in the suburbs for me to walk anywhere safe, especially if I'm going to take my stuff.

Which reminds me: I need to pack. I may never see the inside of this house again; I need to get all my belongings together. So maybe the first step is—

No, wait. The first thing I need to do to get out of this mess is call Tori. She'll come pick me up and be my second brain so I don't forget anything. She'll make sure I do all of this in the best order and get everything taken care of to extricate myself safely. I'm not thinking straight right now.

In fact, maybe she should write this action list for me.

I am definitely forgetting things already.

Let's start over.

1. Call Tori.

I'm, like, 80% sure she'll believe me that this is unten-able. That I mean it this time. Or, really, maybe I've just been fooling myself for six years that no one can tell how bad it's gotten, and Tori will have been waiting for this very phone call. Maybe she's been expecting the breakup for months. Maybe she's already guessed about the thrown glasses. The hole in the wall. The contempt and the threats and the gaslighting and manipulations.

For all I know, that's why Tori has stuck around so long. To be my support when I'm finally ready to leave.

And—god, I just made myself cry again thinking about it. The idea that my cousin, who I rarely got to see as a kid, would randomly move to our town and put up with the insults and sarcasm from my wife for years, would go out of her way to check on me, and invite me to things without Molly, would make sure that our fridge had the basics in it when Molly quit her fifth job in eight months and I could barely keep the utilities on. All because she saw what was happening and was waiting for me to be ready to get out of this.

Well, I'm ready, Tori, and I know that you're my best chance at an escape.

So. First step is to call Tori and . . . and admit that I can't handle this by myself.

(Crying harder now. Goddammit.)

Call Tori and tell her all about Molly screaming at me in the middle of the street this morning. In front of neigh-bors. In front of law enforcement, even.

Step one: call Tori and ask for help.

Step two . . . do whatever she thinks I should do next.

In the meantime, what else do I need to remember to do? My brain is scattered. I can barely remember how to make a decision for myself. I'm still shaking from our fight this morning.

Pack?

I wish I had done laundry more recently.

I wonder where my passport is.

I wonder where my birth certificate is. My Social Security card. Didn't Molly put that stuff in a fireproof box in the closet? I need to find that. I hope she wasn't lying about where she put it.

I'll need to empty the joint bank account, or at least withdraw half of the money in there. Not that there's much after her constant spending and complete inability to hold a job. The only money I've managed to squirrel away is whatever tiny percentage that transfers automatically to my 401(k) before it even hits the bank account.

Molly is still the beneficiary of my retirement account; I wonder how hard it will be to change that.

Without Molly spending all our money, maybe I can finally afford to get out from under all the debt she has brought on us.

But first I need to get another car, and I have no idea how I am ever going to be able to pay for that.

I cannot believe she did this to us. To me.

I cannot believe I let her.

I can't think about that right now. Berating myself for the past or worrying about too far in the future will just paralyze me, and that would be the end of that. I need to focus on what my very next step is.

I need to call Tori, because I need her level-headedness, but also because I need her car.

I cannot believe Molly totaled the car.

My car.

That was the beginning of the end for me, actually. I can put up with a lot, but at some point, the exhaustion of survival, of keeping the bills paid—on top of everything else—is just one thing too many.

Over the years there have already been so many different times when Molly blamed me, or she foisted some problem on me or picked a fight with someone else and then demanded I stand up for her. Hell, it's no wonder I started getting gray hair just six months after I met her. But when pressed, she'd always have such a good reason for doing the things she did. She could always come up with all kinds of justifications for why something was not her fault or why she was the victim or why she needed me to take care of her.

And I fell for it for so long.

It's ridiculous the things we will put up with just to feel that little glow of what we think is love and attention.

This morning, though . . . I couldn't do it anymore. She pushed me once too far, and now I would rather be homeless than spend one more second in that woman's chaos.

I'm so tired of spending day after day just barely hanging on.

This morning, I had to leave work in the middle of my shift—not for the first time—to come rescue Molly. She knows she should not be calling my office unless it's an emergency, so when the phone rang and I recognized her sobbing on the other end, I of course thought the worst. In the past, she's called me from the emergency room after she fainted at work; she's called me from the back of a police car—the only place she claimed to feel safe after thinking someone was breaking into our house in the middle of the day.

"What is it?" I asked, when I recognized her sobs. "What happened?"

"The car . . . I got in a wreck," she gasped out.

"Oh my god, are you okay? Are you hurt? Tell me where you are, I'll be right there."

She'd been driving the new car—the new car that we (I) bought in my name (because her credit is so bad)—while I drove the beat-up hand-me-down Honda from her parents. When we got the new Jetta last year, Molly had been ecstatic. She picked the color. She makes sure there's room in the garage for it. She's even kept it clean (which was a surprise to me, given how carelessly she treats the rest of her things). And—in what should not have been a surprise to me—has come up with an excuse for her to drive it as often as she could, all while I continued to make all the payments on it. This morning, she insisted that she needed to drive the Jetta so she could make a good impression for her job interview. Truthfully, I was pleasantly surprised she hadn't found some excuse to back out of the appointment, so I went along with it. What did it matter what car I drove to work?

And now my new car is wrecked.

"I'm on Colonial Avenue," she said.

I thought I had misheard her.

"Colonial? Like . . . two blocks from home?"

"Hurry," she said, not answering. "The other driver already called the police, and I don't want to do this by myself. I don't know where the insurance information is either, so I need you to take care of that."

"All right. All right, yeah. I'll be there as soon as I can. I love you."

But she had already hung up. And when I raised my head again, my boss was looking at me with such frustration and disappointment that I wished I could have kept Molly on the phone longer. Asked her if she could call her mother—who never failed to jump at the chance to take care of her only child, especially if it meant showing me up. But it was too late for that. My wife was expecting me, and there was nothing I could do but leave work in the middle of the morning to rescue her.

"I'll be back as soon as I can," I told him as I gathered my things.

"It's Molly again, isn't it?" he said.

I could only nod and apologize on my way out the door.

Colonial Avenue is between my work and our home.

No—no longer my home. Was it ever, really? The place belongs to Molly's mother, who rents it out to us (rent that I pay entirely). Which is why I really need to make sure I get everything of mine that has value when I leave this afternoon. There is every chance that neither of them will let me back here.

The whole drive back home this morning, I was so worried about Molly. How could she have gotten in a wreck so close to home? The speed limit on Colonial is twenty-five.

When I turned the corner into our neighborhood and saw my beautiful white, new car in the middle of the street with the passenger side hood crushed, my heart dropped. It was literally caved in at least a foot. Even after hearing her explanation, I still don't understand how she could have possibly done so much damage while driving on a quiet, residential street. A cul-de-sac, no less.

I was more confused than ever.

I had barely parked—hadn't even undone my seatbelt—before Molly was at my door and spluttering out all her excuses and justifications.

"My shoe got stuck! I don't know what happened! If you had just driven me to the interview like I asked you to, this wouldn't have happened!"

"Do *you* have the insurance?" the older man standing next to the car yelled at me.

"Whoa. Wait." I always try to speak calmly to Molly, like she's a fragile puppy who needs to be kept calm; in that moment, with several people talking at me, it was quite difficult. Neighbors? Passengers? It was all chaos. "Start at the beginning."

"Your wife there hit my *parked* car," the old man yelled. "Must've been doing fifty miles per hour down this street."

I looked at Molly, shocked. "Is that true? Babe, come on . . ."

"It wasn't fifty," she protested. "But I was looking down at my phone, and my flip-flop, um, came off? Stuck under the brake, maybe? And—"

"You wore flip-flops to your interview?" I looked down at what she was wearing and realized there was no way she actually went to the job interview that morning.

"I was running errands and was coming home to change. The interview is in ten minutes, so I need to take the other car to do it."

I was stunned. Exhausted. I suddenly wanted to cry

from the mountain of mess that had just been dropped on top of me.

From behind us came the brief beep of a police car's siren, and I turned to see an officer park along the curb behind me.

"Babe, you can't go," I said, trying to be gentle. "Maybe they'll let you reschedule the interview, but you have to be here for the police report so it's not considered a hit-and-run."

"Just tell them you were driving," she said dismissively. It was unnerving how calm she was in the midst of all this. "Give me the keys."

She held out her hand, waiting expectantly for me to once again acquiesce, once again clean up her mess and defend her to strangers and put my own life on hold for her. Once again expecting me to somehow figure out how to keep my job so we can pay our bills while she flits about destroying people's lives with every choice.

"I'm not going to give you the keys."

"Give me the fucking keys," she said, her voice rising, her eyes burning at me. "It's *your fault* I was on the road in the first place! You can't even take care of our family, so *I* have to be out here fucking begging for any job just so we can eat! Fuck *off* with that shit and give me the keys. You wanted the new car in your name so badly? Fine. This is your mess to take care of."

I flinched under her shouting, frozen once again in the face of her hair-trigger temper.

The police officer, a white man whose tired expression and age made me think he might be the dad of young children, approached the old Honda. I was still sitting in the driver's seat, because Molly had crowded me immediately upon my own arrival.

"Everything all right here?" he asked pointedly, looking to Molly. "Who wants to tell me what happened?"

"Yes, Officer," the old man said loudly, crossing the pavement to come join the rest of the group. "My truck was just parked in front of my house, and that woman hit it with her car."

It felt like everyone was crowding in on me; Molly wasn't giving me any space to even think about what needed to be done, let alone get out of the car.

"Is that true, ma'am?" the officer asked my wife.

She looked at me, eyes boring into mine. I knew what she wanted—she wasn't answering because she wanted me to take the blame for it. But given that I was still sitting in the driver's seat of a totally different vehicle, I had no idea how she expected that lie to work.

"It's true," I said.

The look of pure venom she gave me at that said it all: she intended to make me regret that statement.

I knew it. And she knew I knew it.

I was afraid of her for a moment—but, more than that, I was tired. I was tired of being afraid of her and tired of finding excuses for letting this tyrant run my life.

Love is not enough. And right now, I'm not even sure the person I've loved all these years is real. Maybe I imagined her. Maybe I cobbled her together with all the lies and justifications that Molly fed me.

I'm still afraid of her. I know what she's capable of. But I'm more exhausted than scared at this point. I'm already at my lowest.

This morning, with the police officer on one side

asking questions and Molly on the other feeding me lies to answer, for the first time in my life I preferred talking to the former.

I cannot let Molly know where I am going. If she got wind of any of this before I'm ready, she would enlist every single person in our life to convince me that I am being a monster. She's already trying to punish me, and this is only going to make it worse. She'll pull out every single tactic that she has ever tried and fling them all at me.

If today's mess did nothing else, it finally showed me that I cannot allow her a single inch, or I will lose myself completely.

I miss who I used to be before I met Molly.

Maybe that's another reason having Tori around has been helpful. We're about the same age, and though we only saw each other for holidays when we were growing up, we were inseparable for those few days each year. She knew me back when I was happy. When I was myself and dreaming big goals, instead of now, when I'm barely surviving.

She remembers me before Molly took over my entire life.

I need that anchor right now. Without it, I don't know if I have the strength to pull myself out of this destructive whirlpool that is my marriage.

All right, then. Call Tori to come pick me up (first step) and help me pack (second step), and then (third?) help me figure out what to do next.

Once Tori picks me up—and we're at a safe distance—stop sharing my phone location with Molly.

Block her number. Block her on social media.

Block her mother.

Block all her friends who never really included me in their lives anyway.

Send an email with the news and tell her . . . what? Not my contact information. And probably not any kind of separation agreement, suggestions, or promises. I don't want to owe her any more than I can possibly get away with, and I am certain that anything I put in writing she will be able to spin in her favor. And I definitely don't want to give her Tori's contact information and inflict all of that on my cousin. (Maybe have Tori block her too?)

I really should not be doing this by myself.

So maybe don't send Molly an email or anything, maybe . . .

Find a lawyer?

No, wait. Does Tori know a lawyer?

I'm going to need a lawyer.

I'm going to need a damn good lawyer.

How am I going to pay for a lawyer?

Okay, add to the list . . . get a second job? If I'm able to get another car, maybe I could drive for Uber or Door-Dash, or something where she won't be able to just show up at my work? She is absolutely the type to charm some well-meaning mutual friend to find out where I've been. "Just checking in. Hope everything's okay." And then showing up at my place of work to harass me.

Oh, god, I just remembered my high school girlfriend did that. I haven't thought about Sasha in years. She wasn't exactly, officially, my girlfriend. More like a best-friend-who-I-made-out-with-when-we-had-sleepovers. But one night, when she was mad about my making plans with band friends without her, Sasha showed up at my nights-and-weekends job at the mall movie theater and screamed at me. Like, sobbing, cruel, insulting accusations screamed at me. She made such a scene that people who had been eating in the food court came to see what all the fuss was about. At least five people asked for refunds on their movie tickets because of it.

She got me fired.

Now, at this age, I can't afford to get fired. I can't take a second job where Molly could show up at any second and scream at me, and I can't risk interviewing anywhere in this town, in case Molly is still pretending to job-hunt too.

She's totally going to try to get me fired. I don't even have a second job yet and I already know I've lost it.

Although, now that I've thought through all of this, it seems clear that I should wait to get a second job *after* our divorce is finalized, so she can't claim any part of those wages. If Molly gets awarded any kind of spousal support, I'm just—

I'm never going to get out from under this. I'm never going to get away from her.

And now I'm crying again. This all feels so . . . hopeless.

What is the point in even trying? She's relentless when she feels like she's been wronged.

What if she just never stops? What if she never lets up, forever trying to manipulate me and to squeeze as much as she can out of me? What if this is just my life now, moving from one location to another to outrun my ex-wife?

Oh, god, I really need to call Tori. If nothing else, she can help keep me from catastrophizing.

In the meantime, I need to remind myself that this is not actually *completely* hopeless. The best thing I can hope for is that Molly meets someone else as soon as possible and transfers all her controlling and attention and needing to that person.

Dear god, let that be soon.

I suppose it's actually a blessing that as soon as it was clear to Molly that I wasn't going to lie to the police for her, she called her mother.

She called her mother, who of course showed up in minutes to protect her baby girl when the spouse failed just like she always said would happen. She showed up, and they had a whispered consultation, before my mother-in-law (ignoring me completely) took over talking to the police officer on her daughter's behalf.

Molly had stopped talking to me by then, too. Just stood with her arms crossed over her chest by her mom. Not even deigning to glance at me.

And . . . it was a relief.

The moment I realized I was relieved that my wife wasn't speaking to me, relieved that I was no longer expected to throw myself on this grenade that she'd tossed in the first place—

That was the moment I realized I needed to be done with all of it.

It's not the first time she has punished me for not magically bending reality to match what she wants. Molly is an expert at the silent treatment, which is usually what she starts with. When we first started dating, I was constantly anxious, wondering what I had done wrong, wondering what I could do to get her to forgive me. As the years went on, though, I slowly realized that whatever prompted her silent pouting was never consistent. I could react to one of her requests the exact same way three times in a row, and I'd get three different responses.

(Of course, if I pointed that out, she'd have plenty of justifications, and just my suggesting as much would then prompt another silent treatment.)

All right. Okay, then.

I . . . I'm actually starting to feel a little bit more hopeful now.

I didn't think that was possible.

But maybe—*maybe*—getting Molly out of my life, even if she keeps trying to sabotage it, will give me the space and calm I need to finally get out of this survival mode I've been in for the last six years.

I just have to get away from her. *That* is the real first step. I need to disconnect entirely, which is no easy feat, given the fact that she's entwined every part of our lives together practically since we met.

I don't know where to even start.

I'm so lost.

Is this the kind of thing I could google?

No. I should just call Tori. Besides, over the phone is better. Then there's no electronic trail Molly can follow. Just in case.

Yes. Tori will know what to do. She can help me figure out what I need to do first. What I need to pack.

Crap, I need to pack something. A go-bag of some kind. What do people put in those things? Do we have any empty boxes in the garage?

I just checked my wallet: $43 in cash. Not nearly enough.

The joint account holds $2,833, almost half of which

is going to be gone any day when the rent check—to Molly's mother—clears. I can probably take out four or five hundred before she notices. How much does the ATM let me take out at once? Then at least I'll have cash.

Tori can drive me by the ATM after she picks me up.

My solo bank account is basically empty. I get my paycheck and then almost every single cent gets transferred to the joint bank account for bills, and (I realize now) so Molly can have more control over it. Over the last year I've been able to hold back a bit every month to save up for gifts and things, but that's all gone now.

Only a couple weeks ago, I spent about a thousand dollars on Molly. Grand gesture or whatever. She insisted that we do something big and important and romantic for Valentine's Day, and then—big surprise—I was the only one who actually made an effort. I took her out to dinner at the nicest restaurant in town, and then theater tickets, and somehow it still prompted snide comments about it just being the regional tour, not an actual Broadway show.

For being bisexual, she sure is weirdly obsessed with gender roles where she gets to be the princess and I have to be the provider. What did I get for Valentine's Day? Oh, I got to see her in lingerie—that *I* bought. Nice, but not even close to the same.

(And this is where I remember Tori pointed out that exact thing to me within the first few months Molly and I were dating. I owe her an apology. I know she'll still take my call and help me either way, but I should really give her a chance to say "I told you so.")

Back to the first step.

Siri, call Tori.

Gravity

Deep breath.

From this vantage it looks far steeper than he thought.

He shifts his weight, flexing his toes inside his shoes as he attempts to get a better grip on the board. The sandpaper-like surface is practically brand new.

If he falls off, it won't be the board's fault.

Keeping one foot on the concrete, he bounces lightly, weighing what he has to do next, hyping himself up for the big leap.

One more deep breath as he scans the surface of the road, looking out for sticks, pebbles, anything that might be an obstacle for the hard, plastic wheels.

He lifts his foot, shifting his weight forward on the board to nudge those wheels into motion. The nose dips as the long driveway descends.

Both feet on the board now.

The speed picks up rapidly.

Leaning back to keep the balance, to keep from falling forward on his head.

So much steeper than he'd expected.

Gaze focused on the low row of shrubs at the foot of the hill.

Shifting his weight the tiniest amount to maintain his trajectory.

The wind whipping at his face, tears streaming from his eyes in the dry air.

Holding his arms out to balance himself.

Knees bent, squatting carefully to anchor himself to the board.

Wheels rattling. Board vibrating. Heart pounding.

The thrill is intense.

Overwhelming.

He yields to the terrifying delight, the blur of colors streaks past him, and closes his eyes.

There is no slowing down, no turning to either side. The only thing he can do is keep his balance. He can manage to hang on to this wild ride, or he can bail.

It's over almost as soon as it begins.

Feeling the slightest bit of leveling out as he reaches the bottom of the hill, he opens his eyes.

The front wheels hit the almost imperceptible—*almost*—lip of concrete and the whole board jolts.

His hard-fought balance upends.

He soars through the air, as gravity lets go of him.

For just a brief moment he forgets what is on the other side of that fall. There is nothing that can ruin this euphoric rush of flight.

Geese

Silhouettes in the fog, crouched close to the grass, with angles in unexpected places.

The wide expanse of unbroken field surrounding the high school dips down, a short hill before the neighboring business. Occasionally teenage athletes will fill that grassy sea, stretching before a run or cooling down after.

Now, however, early on a Saturday morning, the foggy blanket covering the field renders the silhouettes unidentifiable.

The Divine Current

"Have you seen Star?"

As she strode through the early morning crowd, Phoenix asked the question over and over, to every person she met, even murmuring it to herself when there was no one else in hearing. Star had been supposed to meet her that morning before dawn, out at the edge of the meadow by the third well, but hadn't showed. Phoenix waited for nearly twenty minutes, so long that she was afraid she'd be missed, afraid that she'd have to answer awkward questions and come up with more lies about where she'd been. When she finally accepted the fact that Star would not be meeting her, she ran back to the main part of the compound, hurrying to start her tasks for the day so no one would suspect anything.

Phoenix didn't want to assume the worst, but at this point it felt like the worst could be the most reasonable interpretation.

She pushed between the dirty flaps of the canvas tent, following the others. The community's mess tent was busy, with most of the Divine Current eager to get through breakfast so they could begin their workday. Efficient and focused use of their energy was one of the key tenets of the community, almost to the point of becoming competitive. At the height of summer as it was, even with more than thirteen hours of daylight there were still more than enough chores to keep every member of the fifty-seven-person compound busy.

Phoenix shuffled to the food-serving table, picked up her bowl, and got in line behind the sisters from Indiana that had joined only the week before.

"Have you seen Star?" she asked Nova, as the latter spooned oatmeal into a bowl for her.

Nova was an older woman, with wild hair that never seemed to stay in whatever bun or braid was forced upon it. She was a good six inches shorter than Phoenix, old enough to be the Conduit's mother, and had been part of the community almost since the beginning. She often presided over meals, claiming that it nourished her to nourish others.

"I saw her last night," she said, handing over Phoenix's cardboard-tasting breakfast. For all the honey and fruit the community harvested from the compound and surrounding areas, she would never understand why they didn't get to indulge in even a little bit of that with breakfast. Nova leaned in close for her next reveal. "I think I saw her leaving Glint's tent, but I won't tell anyone else that."

Phoenix's eyes went wide. She plastered a smile on her face. "Oh, yeah. Good thinking. Thanks."

Nova nodded, winked, and then turned to the teenage boy behind Phoenix in line.

When Phoenix turned toward the rest of the tent, she noticed that nearly every seat was taken. This was later than she usually ate breakfast, preferring to be out of the mess tent before most people were even awake. With her cooling bowl in one hand, she grabbed a napkin and spoon from the nearby station and took her breakfast outside.

More members of the Divine Current were streaming toward the mess tent for their own breakfasts. Phoenix nodded, smiled, greeted them all, even as she looked past them for signs of Star. If she had been in Glint's tent last night, perhaps she had just overslept this morning and their plan to run away from this mysterious place full of overbearing people was still in play.

"Ugh. Oatmeal again. I don't know if I can stomach that."

Phoenix whirled around to see Star standing just behind her. "Where did you come from? I've been looking for you."

"Bathroom," she said with a sigh.

Phoenix was surprised and irritated at her friend's nonchalance. "I thought we were leaving," she insisted in a whisper, yanking Star's arm to pull her to the side, away from the others walking toward the mess tent. "You were supposed to meet me this morning."

"I know." She looked around, smiling automatically at the pair of young women passing nearby. "We're not *leaving*, though, right? We're just . . . talking about it?"

Phoenix looked at her, aghast, and shook her head. "What— But— Fine. Yeah. Not leaving *yet*. But the 'talking about it' part is essential planning for the actual *leaving* part."

"I *know*," Star said again.

"Then why didn't you meet me?"

Her friend looked terrified, and Phoenix suddenly knew that something had changed in the last twelve hours. Something major. Something that she would not be able to talk Star through.

"Star?"

Her friend shook off her fear and offered her a bright smile, though she seemed to have tears in her eyes.

"I just . . . I *can't*, Phee. I can't. I don't have anywhere to go *to*." She'd dropped her whisper even quieter, as though ashamed to admit this.

"But . . ." Phoenix groaned, ready to cry herself. "We can figure it out. I think I can call my grandmother, and she won't hang up on me. And even if not, we're smart and strong and . . . God, you know that we can do it, Star. As long as we're together. We just need to get away from this place and we can figure it out. We'll be fine. We'll be *good*, even. Better than here."

"It's not that easy."

"It can be—"

"I'm *pregnant!*"

Phoenix's stomach dropped. Two twenty-something girls on their own in 1970 America was one thing, but add a baby to that? She thought quickly, trying to recalibrate her plans, to find a new angle of reassurance and optimism. But Star continued.

"Glint is so excited about the baby. And he thinks that the community here is a much better place for us to raise a child than out there. We have food here, Phee. Astral is a midwife. Papa Drake takes care of us."

It was then Phoenix knew she would never convince

Star to leave. The community's leader, Israel Drake—Papa Drake, the Conduit—claimed in all his sermons that he alone could care for them, he alone could intercede on their behalf with God. It was Star who had first pointed out the cracks in his façade, and if she now, so suddenly, was choosing to believe him wholeheartedly, there was nothing Phoenix could do or say to change that.

"All right," she said miserably. "I understand. A baby does change things."

Both of the women knew—though neither would say it out loud—that the chances of Star and Glint actually getting to be parents to this child were slim. While Drake encouraged his followers to multiply, preferring the women to always be pregnant or nursing, he also espoused a belief in community living. "It takes a village to raise a child" and all that. When Phoenix had first arrived, she'd been assigned to the nursery to care for the babies that other women had borne.

What would most likely happen was that Star would have her baby, get the six weeks' maternity leave with it that Drake allowed, and then have to return to her job in the barn, taking better care of the community's pigs and chickens than she did her own child. From then on, it would be no-contact with the child. She'd become miserable again, looking for a way out but not wanting to leave her child behind, until she got pregnant and the cycle started all over again.

It broke Phoenix's heart, and it was seeing this same story throughout the entire community over and over which made it so difficult for her to decide to leave all of the rest of her friends to this fate. But the longer she was here, the more she saw the way Israel Drake took over every aspect of their life, the more she realized that this was not the place for her. She would hate to leave the children behind, but she had to hope that the other adults would look after them.

Surely Drake would not actually hurt any of them. His controlling was the worst that she'd seen, but she couldn't think it would get worse.

Phoenix had to believe that, or she'd never get free herself.

Turning back to Star, she said with a sigh, "You won't tell anyone of my plans, though, will you?"

Star shook her head and smiled sadly. "I don't even *know* your plans. But, no, I'll maintain my ignorance if you decide to go without me. I hope you'll rethink this, though. We're safe and happy here, Phee . . . part of something bigger than us. You know what the Conduit says about what we're building here. I'm willing to let my choices be for the community instead of just myself . . . aren't you?"

"I'll think about it," Phoenix lied. "But don't worry about me. Take care of yourself. Did you eat yet?"

Star put a hand to her stomach self-consciously. "My morning sickness is making that near impossible. I did tell Ember I was on my way to breakfast, though, so I should go do that before she sends someone after me."

"Yeah, go do that. Of course."

She didn't know what else to say. All the arguments she had made in the preceding weeks weren't going to make any difference now, and between Glint and the rest of the community, there was nothing Phoenix could offer Star that she couldn't find elsewhere.

Watching her friend walk toward the mess tent,

Phoenix mechanically put a spoonful of her own breakfast in her mouth. It was mediocre at best, but it would give her energy that she needed to get through the day.

She was on her own.

When the rising sun crested over the trees, Phoenix realized how late in the morning it was. She was behind on the chores she needed to complete, and if she wasn't running away from the compound right that moment, she needed to at least keep up a semblance of continuity. She shoveled the rest of her breakfast down, leaving the dirty dish and heading back out to the tent where she worked.

Striding through the tent city, Phoenix tried to manufacture an expression of unconcern. That the only thing on her mind was the classwork she needed to attend to and not the on-going question of how and when she was going to escape this place without getting caught and brought back.

Among the members of the Divine Current, Phoenix was an outlier in more ways than one. Nearly every other person she'd talked to at any length had stories of being kicked out by their parents, hooked on heroin, jailed for petty theft. It was not a coincidence that when Israel Drake offered them a home and his approval, they'd lunged for it.

She, on the other hand, had an uneasy relationship with her grandparents who raised her, and that was where the similarities ended. She had a semester of college under her belt, no arrest record, and the hardest drug she'd ever done was weed. While everyone else, it seemed, came to Drake because they had nowhere else to go, she had come here because she'd been running away from the mundanity of the life in which she'd found herself.

When she'd first arrived she'd felt so grateful for the opportunity. Here she'd found friends, support, concern, but also adventure. She was an only child and had never lived with anyone other than her grandparents. She'd never even been on a farm, and the rumors of the uranium mine somewhere on the compound had been enough to make her eyes as wide as saucers. The Divine Current was a whole new world, and she drank it up.

Papa Drake could be inspiring, feeding them visions of a future with all the divine energy required to run the world, and the community's role in that future, but really it had been the women surrounding him who had made the most difference to Phoenix. Their companionship had been so healing for her that now, eleven months later, she could see her own flaws better. She could see her folly in running away from the life in which she'd grown up. She could see that the Divine Current was not the place for her. Whatever their future might be—and some part of her still believed in that promised future—she would not be part of it.

She could see that she needed to leave.

That was not going to be easy, however. It had not been an exaggeration that Star and Phoenix had needed to keep even any conversations about leaving the compound secret. While ostensibly the members of the Divine Current could go whenever they wanted, in practice Drake—the Conduit—controlled their every movement. He directed their energy; he made all their choices.

Because she was possibly the only person in the entire community with any post-high-school education, not long after Phoenix arrived she had been assigned to be the teacher for the small, but growing, collection of children the community was raising. The first couple of weeks were difficult and confusing for her, as she tried to understand the limited curriculum Drake had designed, combined with the wide range of ages she was expected to teach. There was Zephyr, twelve years old and the only child of new member Volt, all the way down to Blaze, three years old and first-generation, born within the Divine Circuit, whose father was unknown.

But after those first two weeks—and some internal compromises—Phoenix got a handle on it. She was expected to clean and reset the learning environment each morning, which would clear the energy and create new channels for knowledge. In other words, to be ready for the fifteen children to begin classwork at nine.

As she'd finished her breakfast and started toward the school tent, Phoenix realized she was going to be late. She hurried toward the tent where her school lessons were held, hoping that she wasn't so late that there would be children waiting for her when she got there. She would just have to hope that she had a chance throughout the morning to do the resetting that she should have done before class started.

As she darted around the side of the tent to the entrance, she stopped short at what was waiting for her.

Israel Drake, the leader and Conduit of the Divine Current, stood with his hands clasped in front of him, waiting patiently, presumably for Phoenix herself. He wore his usual all-white linen attire, pants and button-up shirt with delicate silver thread that could only be seen in certain lights. His bald head was bare, opening his crown chakra to the universe.

Phoenix stopped short, her mouth falling open in shock.

What was he doing here?

She had not had a conversation with him in months, ever since she'd been asked to take over the education. While most members of the Divine Current would kill (some literally) for an opportunity for this man's attention, whenever Phoenix felt herself under his gaze she wondered all over again how he had gotten to where he was. She felt unsettled, but she could not let him see that.

"Papa Drake," she said, composing herself and closing the distance between them. "I'm honored."

She bowed her head slightly, the balance between showing this man respect and pretending he was just like everyone else was delicate. Even as he accepted her deference, he insisted all were equal.

"Phoenix Bright, my child," he said formally.

It was the name he himself had chosen for her when she joined the community. There had been a ceremony and everything, and while Phoenix had gotten used to her new name, hearing it in his unctuous voice made her skin crawl. She had known it was time for her to leave the compound when she was no longer as enamored with Drake as she'd once been.

"Can I be of service?" she asked, suppressing the impulse to look around, to check that none of the children had arrived yet.

"Nova mentioned that lessons this week were about the constellations, so I thought I would sit in with you. I'm sure the children will have questions, and I want you to feel supported in this shaping of our young minds."

"Oh." Phoenix forced a brighter smile. "Thank you.

Please don't think me ungrateful, but I don't wish to be a distraction from what must be your more important duties."

"There is nothing more important than strengthening these children's connection to the celestial energy of the heavens."

"Of course." She pushed open the flap of canvas. "Please allow me, Conduit."

Phoenix ducked her head to walk into the tent—a canvas canopy—then stood up straight, hyper-aware of her posture as the leader of the Divine Current followed her inside. Despite his insincere protests to the contrary, everyone in the community knew that Drake's word was law, and his temperament was unpredictable. If he decided he needed to sit in on her class today for the first time ever, there wasn't anything she could do to dissuade him.

"Students should be here any minute," she said. "I don't have a desk; I apologize that I cannot offer you a more appropriate place to sit."

"Please, Phoenix Bright," he said, waving his hand dismissively. "I require no special treatment."

She did not have a chance to respond before the first of her students streamed in. As she greeted them each in turn, Phoenix hoped that Drake was not so much of an excessive controller to recognize what she had left undone that morning.

There was a handful of chairs under the canopy—there'd been more previously, but those had been "borrowed" and never returned—but most of the students found seats on blankets or bean bag chairs scattered around the tent. Phoenix had long ago stopped trying to manage where the children sat, stopped trying to keep similar-aged kids together. Despite the tight control Drake wielded over much of their lives, things were still chaotic on the compound. Boys would not come to class for weeks at a time because it was harvest season, or girls would have to leave in the middle of a lesson to wait on Papa Drake and some esteemed guest he was entertaining in The House. She simply did her best with whoever showed up each day, and let the elders of the Divine Current worry about what that meant for the community long-term.

"Good morning, good morning," she called out to the assembled students. She counted thirteen for today, class's official start time having passed ten minutes earlier. "As you can see, we have a special guest this morning"—she gestured at Drake—"and I know he would love to see your best behavior, your most brilliant questions. Today, class, we're going to be talking about constellations. Who can tell me what that means?"

She wished she'd had a chance to look over the lesson plan again, but in the chaos of changed plans with Star and then Drake showing up unannounced, Phoenix would have to go off of memory. There was a loose schedule of topics that Drake had written down the previous year, leaving generous gaps in how exactly to cover those topics. She usually appreciated the lack of oversight, but with Drake himself sitting in the back of the room, she was not able to veer from his structure.

As she skimmed quickly through the thin folder of lesson guidance, Phoenix lamented the fact that these kids were growing up not just without desks and chairs or a proper teacher, but also without books, without pen and paper. As far as she had been able to assess, all of the children seven years and older could read, but she still wasn't sure how well any of them could write, and she'd been teaching them for eight months.

But when she looked back up at the class, her eyes fell on Israel Drake, who seemed to be watching her closely. This whole setup seemed to be exactly what he had in mind, even to giving her as few resources as possible to educate them. One more way the Conduit was making everyone dependent on him.

She was reminded of her own childhood. She'd been orphaned at age eight, and in the chaos of the funerals and moving a state over to live with her grandparents, she'd missed enough school that she'd had to be held back a year. Though she'd been given all the chances the adults around her could manage, she had strong memories of being distraught at the thought that she would be left behind, that she'd miss some important life skill that everyone else had learned.

She could not imagine how the children of the Divine Current might feel.

Another unfortunate consequence of living in this community, she realized, was that the children likely didn't even know they could have better than this.

Before she could start the lesson, Ash had taken her encouragement to heart and raised his hand.

"Yes?"

"I have a question about the stars," he said.

He was eleven years old, and had been brought into the community with his older sister, the pair found begging on the streets of Denver late last fall, both given new names and jobs on the compound. They'd been brought in just before the first snows hit, and Ash had taken to the free spirit of the community like a duck to water. It was no surprise to Phoenix that he now wanted to impress Papa Drake with his own brilliant question.

"What's your question?"

"How did the souls get up in the sky?"

Phoenix frowned, then half smiled, unsure if Ash was serious or not, before recalling what Drake had alluded to in a sermon a month or so earlier.

"Why would you ask that?" she asked cautiously.

"Because Papa Drake says"—he glanced at the older man sitting quietly in the corner—"that when we die we become stars. Celestial energy. And the stars become galaxies, so we'll all have a bunch of planets around us after we die. And I was just wondering how we get from here to there, since it's not like we ever see people floating up, you know?"

Phoenix had to bite the inside of her cheek to keep herself from screaming in frustration. She turned her back to the students and busied herself with flipping through the folder of lesson notes to avoid having to look at them. If Drake had not been sitting there, would she be brave enough to contradict his teachings?

"Um, well, you know, Ash, that's a good question. And maybe Papa Drake can address it in future lessons. I'm not sure I understand the exact mechanics of it myself."

She turned around to face the class again, having calmed her anger as well as possible. Though not brave enough to look at Drake while she said this, Phoenix realized that she was brave enough to not give in to his warped ideas of the world any longer.

It was no longer just about Phoenix getting away to save herself. She had to report this to the police. She had to get someone in here to stop it. These children were being lied to, and not only was she allowing it, but she was one of the prime mouthpieces for those lies. At best, they were missing out on the life skills they'd need as adults. And at the worst?

Not anymore.

She'd make her escape that night, and then, maybe, somehow, something could be done for these kids.

"For now, though," she continued, "let's focus on the lesson about the stars that Papa Drake was so wise to craft for us."

For the rest of the day, she had the children memorizing the constellations that they'd see over the following six months. Without paper to write on, she had them replicating the constellations with their fingers in the dirt. Papa Drake set a great store on the ancient interpretations of the constellations, weaving the Egyptians and Greeks throughout his sermons when he could, likening himself to the great thinkers of history.

Fortunately, all Phoenix had to teach the kids was what the constellations looked like. Any further brainwashing was not part of what was expected of her.

Drake left after a couple hours, not bothering to say anything to Phoenix before he did so. She had no idea if he was pleased with her teaching or now planned to replace her. There was no telling with him, his whims were unpredictable and, she suspected, influenced by whatever drug he had recently binged on or whatever personal slights he felt in the moment.

As she said goodbye to the children at the end of the

school day, Phoenix felt a sense of grief. If all went as planned that evening, she may not ever be seeing them again. She had to trust that her actions outside of the compound would be more effective than and make up for this inside position as part of the community. Whatever people like Nova or Star wanted to do with their own life was one thing, but the future of these unsuspecting children was quite another.

The first problem, however, was how Phoenix would be able to get away undetected.

When Star had been planning to leave with her, the two women thought they could come up with some reason to go into town together. While Phoenix was in charge of educating the children, Star's primary role in the community was with the farm animals. As such, she occasionally joined the team of public-facing members that sold the vegetables, honey, and fresh eggs the compound produced. It was a flimsy plan—coming up with some reason why Star had to go and *had* to bring Phoenix and only Phoenix—but it was better than nothing.

Now Phoenix had nothing.

No plan, no ally, no ideas.

But, she reminded herself, as only one person, perhaps it would be easier for her to hide. She could just slip away quietly, not have to worry about anyone else being seen or heard. She didn't have many personal possessions, and none that she needed to take with her. If she had to, she could run away with just the clothes on her back, though she hoped she'd have the chance to be slightly more prepared.

The Divine Current compound was in the southwest

of Colorado, a little outside of Telluride and the ski lodges that brought the wealthy to the slopes. Drake had chosen this location in part for its difficulty to get to, surrounded as it was by rugged mountains, and in part for the possibility of uranium mines. There had been rumors and whispers about who really owned the land they were on, but Phoenix had heard nothing for sure. All she knew was there was one gravel road in and out of the compound, and it was a full three miles through meadows and forests before she could even reach a paved road, let alone another person.

She thought—she *hoped*—that if she could get ahold of her grandmother she'd get at least *some* help. If she could get to a town, maybe there'd be a bus ticket waiting for her. After how she'd left things at home, when she found Drake and cut ties with her family, Phoenix knew it would be a difficult conversation if she were to ever go back to them. But now that she'd been here almost a year, humbling herself and eating crow for a tiny bit of help getting out were steps she was more than willing to take.

She had to find a way to call, and then once she knew what kind of help from outside the compound was waiting for her, Phoenix could formulate the rest of her plan.

The only phone on the entire compound was in The House.

The fact that The House had electricity, working plumbing, and a phone at all was a minor miracle, one that Drake was constantly taking credit for. The rest of the community ran on daylight, oil lamps, rain barrels, and well water. When Phoenix had first gotten there she had fallen in love with the romantic, pastoral ideal, enjoying the strength she was building after carrying buckets of water—the "all-natural energy" they were harvesting, according to Drake. It had only taken about six weeks for her to tire of that life. She'd never thought of herself as needing luxury, but modern conveniences were certainly desirable.

Dinner would be ready any moment, and she'd be expected in the mess tent. While breakfast and lunch were more casual, Drake insisted that the entire community eat dinner together. That meant that she would certainly be missed if she did not appear on time, but it also meant that dinner might be her only window of time to sneak into The House and use the phone while the rest of the community were elsewhere.

It was worth the risk.

Phoenix didn't know what other options she had. She had to get into The House, call her grandmother, and ask for help. She had to get out of here quickly, before her distaste for Drake and her lack of commitment to the cause became more obvious. His sudden appearance in her classroom was reason enough for her to worry.

She was overthinking this. She needed to just go for it.

Leaving her scant lesson plans behind, Phoenix made her way through the compound, forcing herself to go at a leisurely pace. She walked past the mess tent, trying to be casual while still staying alert to who was around, what gaps in the security she might see. Before she ran out into the literal wilderness, she wanted to fill a bag with food and water. She had an idea that it was something like twenty or thirty miles to the closest town, but no member of the community ever walked that. It was a bus ride once every week or so.

The House was set apart, the only permanent structure on the land. It was the first thing any new visitor saw if they traveled down the gravel driveway from the main road: a squat, wooden building from the turn of the century and updated only slightly over the decades. Two bedrooms housed Drake's sleeping quarters—always with one or more partners, depending on how he was feeling that night—and his office, where he worked on his sermons and kept track of the organization's finances.

The office was also where the only phone was, or so Phoenix had heard. She'd been as far as the front door of The House, but no farther. It was only some things that Nova had mentioned in passing, fragments in a variety of conversations over several months, that gave Phoenix the knowledge she had.

But because The House was so far set off from the rest of the community, there was no real reason why she should be walking toward it. As she walked more slowly between the tents for sleeping and laundry, she racked her brain for a plausible lie that could get her into The House. She had no idea who might be inside this time of day, if truly everyone reported to the mess tent for dinner, and she could not bear to stay here any longer to do whatever necessary reconnaissance she thought she needed.

It was this or nothing.

And Phoenix had spent too much of her life putting up with nothing to let this continue any longer.

Confident in her ability to come up with something to say if required, she altered her route to take her around the back of The House toward where the primary well was. If she approached from the back, perhaps the windows would be open, or some light source would help her identify if anyone was inside.

Resisting the urge to look around—she didn't want to appear too suspicious if anyone happened to notice her—she walked to the well and busied herself lowering a bucket down to collect water. She barely noticed what she was doing with her hands as she strained her eyes and ears to notice anything going on inside the house. The windows were open, and the movement of curtains fluttering kept drawing her attention.

The sound of women working in the orchard some sixty yards away carried over the flat ground. It was almost like a magic trick, the way sound bounced around in this place. She heard a conversation about needing new shoes, snatches of talk about breakfast that morning, but she could not be completely sure where the sounds were coming from nor who was talking. There were simply too many people, all living practically on top of each other.

But she didn't think any of them were looking her way.

She snuck closer to the open windows at the back of The House, listening hard.

There didn't seem to be anyone inside.

The windows were not quite low enough for her to climb into The House gracefully, which was a shame, because how often were the windows left open with no one inside? Would the front door be unlocked? Phoenix realized she didn't even know if there was a back or side door to The House.

She was running headlong into the void of the unknown.

But stopping was not an option.

Walking around the north side of the house, closer to where more of the sleeping tents were—though those were hopefully empty right now—Phoenix finally gave up any hope of stealth or deception. She was just going to go for it and hope for the best.

She needed to get to that phone.

The House had a tiny front porch, with a rocking chair that appeared so dusty as to not be in regular use. There was a wide front window that looked out toward the gravel drive, and a creaky screen door that showed signs of wear.

After opening the screen, Phoenix paused, holding her breath and listening.

If anyone was inside, now was her last chance to be prepared.

She rapped gently on the door. Nothing.

She tried the handle, which turned easily.

Phoenix had to admit she was surprised. Israel Drake did not seem like the type to leave his private space unlocked and unguarded.

Maybe he was coming right back.

She needed to hurry.

Letting the screen fall shut behind her, Phoenix hurried deeper into the house, not examining the living area, the doorway to what was probably the kitchen, or the hallway that would take her back to the bedroom. From the entryway of The House, she'd easily seen through the doorframe into the first room and Drake's office.

She could *see* the phone from where she stood.

It took all of three long, quick strides for Phoenix to cross the small space and reach the office. One wall was taken up by full bookshelves—which, frankly, surprised her; Drake didn't seem like the type who would willingly seek out other people's knowledge or advice. The opposite wall held a single filing cabinet, but also several haphazardly stacked boxes of paperwork. Curiosity almost got the best of her; Phoenix had so many questions about what kind of records that man would care enough to keep.

But her eyes returned to the black rotary phone situated on the corner of the desk. It was only as she was picking up the handset that she remembered she'd be calling long-distance, and those records could easily be pulled. She paused, wondering if she would be putting her grandmother in danger by calling her from here.

Should she wait until she got to town?

Over the low hum of the dial tone, she heard the floorboards creak suddenly from elsewhere in the house. She dropped the handset in a panic and spun in a half circle, desperately wondering how to escape.

A silhouette darkened the doorway. Light from the front door spilled through and around the squat, wild-haired figure of Nova.

"Phoenix? Did you need something?"

She had already dropped the phone when she'd heard the footsteps, but in her fluster she'd left the handset off the hook, practically dangling off the desk. The dial tone buzzed audibly. To Phoenix's ears it was so loud as to be deafening.

"What are you doing in here?" she asked in a panic.

"What are *you* doing in here?" Nova asked, the barest hint of suspicion in her tone.

Phoenix was silently grateful that she'd never before

given this woman a reason to suspect her. Eleven months of perfect behavior were now paying off.

"I was looking for . . ."

Her eyes searched the bookshelves, desperate for something to spark a believable story.

". . . um . . . a book?"

"A book?" Nova raised her eyebrows. "Any particular book?"

"Right. Yes. Ha!" Phoenix hung up the phone again, trying to appear casual, easy, not as guilty as she clearly was. "This morning Papa Drake observed my class for a few hours, and after he left I thought perhaps he might have a book about the constellations. I've been teaching the children from memory, you see, and I'm afraid that I might be instilling in them incorrect information."

"Did Papa Drake say anything to you about correcting mistakes to what you were teaching?"

"Um . . . no?"

"So you just took it upon yourself to add to his curriculum?"

"Oh." Phoenix swallowed. "When you put it like that, um . . . you're right. You're completely right." She looked around the room again, her eyes falling briefly on the phone as she felt her one chance slipping away. "I should have trusted that Papa Drake made his choices for a reason."

"He makes every choice for a reason."

"Mm-hmm." Phoenix nodded, smiling, her mouth closed, as she tried to edge around Nova to get out of the room. She could not handle having to lie to more people if Drake or someone else showed up. She could not stand to be around these followers any longer than she abso-lutely had to.

"Anyway, now is not the time. We should be at dinner. Come, dear."

Nova put her hand tightly on Phoenix's upper arm, guiding her from the office into the living room and then out the front door of The House. Phoenix almost tripped from the ceaseless pushing and pulling. All while pretending nothing was wrong, that she was embarrassed to have been questioning Drake.

Once they were outside, it took all of her self-control to not just start running down the gravel driveway that stretched out in front of her. She'd never get away if she was seen. Now that Nova had found her doing something even the tiniest bit questionable, any other action she took would be interpreted through that same lens, assuming her judgment had somehow been compromised.

And then Drake would use that as another excuse to exert more control over her.

"You should get to dinner," Nova said, her tone unreadable.

"I will, yeah. Yes, I'm going right there. Are—are you?"

"You interrupted me getting something for Papa Drake's dinner. I'll see you there."

"Right. Yeah. Thanks again," Phoenix said over her shoulder as she hurried toward the mess tent.

She glanced back at Nova once, making sure the older woman wasn't following her.

Phoenix had no intention of going to the mess tent.

It would mean hours overnight without food or water. It would mean hunger and exhaustion and leaving behind everything she had here at the compound. But she was too afraid that her interactions with both Nova and Papa Drake—not to mention Star—might paint a target on her. She had to go—*now*. Now, before things got worse. Now, while everyone was eating and not paying attention and Nova hadn't the opportunity to alert Drake of her behavior.

Whatever difficulty was ahead of her would be nothing compared to what the Divine Current could do to her here.

She wove around the long way, between the school tent and the barn, between the mess tent and the well, sticking to shadows as much as she could while the sun had not yet set completely.

"Phoenix?" someone called through the dusk.

Her heart sank; she had been spotted. But she was already gone, walking faster now, trying not to draw attention to herself by running while people could still see her. Perhaps whoever had called after her would think they were mistaken. Perhaps she could reach the edge of the trees and disappear.

She quickened her pace.

"Do you need help?" the voice called after her.

But Phoenix had put enough space between them that she could pretend she couldn't hear. It broke her heart a little bit, the knowledge that someone here cared enough to make sure she was all right, to offer her help. There was a sense of community and mutual aid that existed here despite Drake's tight control. She had to admit she would miss that.

Turning back to check if she was being followed, Phoenix realized there was a group of four adults, all half-running toward her. Crystal was trying to wave her down, to get her attention.

They were quickly closing the distance.

She had only a moment.

Phoenix ran, picking up her skirts as she sprinted through the tall grass. Her sandals had flown off after only three or four steps. Though she paused to grab them, she did not stop long enough to don them again. On she ran, through the undergrowth. She kept going. Stepping in mud. Grass between her toes. Bruising her heel as she landed on stone after stone, but still she kept running.

After stumbling once or twice, bruising her shoulder on the tree trunk she all but bounced off of, she had to stop to catch her breath. She darted behind one of the wider trees to listen for voices or footsteps or signs of someone following her. Chest heaving, Phoenix closed her eyes to listen. There was rustling in the trees overhead, some in the leaves and brush that covered the forest floor. Were there bears in Colorado?

She swallowed hard and peeked around the tree trunk to look in the direction she'd just come. She couldn't guess how far she'd run, and though she thought—she hoped—she was going in the direction of the main road, in the chaos of escaping maybe she'd veered off.

Her breath was slowing, but her heart still raced. She thought she'd escaped whoever might have tried to stop her, but she was far from in the clear. There were still miles to go, in the dark, without a map or practical shoes or even a swallow of water.

Since she was stopped, Phoenix slipped her sandals back on her feet. There were some cuts she could feel even in the dark, and her first few steps were at a limp, but it was nothing she could not overcome. Or at least ignore. There was far more she was willing to do to get away from Israel Drake if she had to.

Once she'd caught her breath, Phoenix began walking again, checking over her shoulder periodically or pausing to listen from time to time. Minute by minute she became more confident that she'd outrun her pursuers, though she knew if they really wanted to find her all it would take would be to patrol the main road where they had to guess she was headed.

She hoped they did not really want to find her.

She hoped that her failure in answering Ash's question earlier that day had made her undesirable to Drake.

She hoped that all the friends she'd left behind would understand why she'd not felt at home there and would wish her well.

She hoped she'd never find out how great of lengths Drake or his security team went through to bring her back.

The night wore on and so did her steps. Through the tree canopy she could see just enough of the constellations to be able to very roughly gauge her direction. As long as she was going more or less straight, she'd hit the road eventually.

Hours went by. Her steps grew slower. Her body grew tired. Every so often she would look up through the trees to roughly estimate whether or not she was heading in the right direction. On one such of these pauses, Phoenix realized the trees were thinning. It was too dark to be certain, but she thought perhaps the road was up ahead.

After hours of trudging, she found strength again to hurry ahead.

In moments, she had stepped out of the trees onto the narrow shoulder of the wide, paved road. Phoenix looked both directions but saw no lights, no movement, no street signs. Nothing at all that indicated where she was or which direction she should be going.

But she had found it.

She was off the compound.

If she could get away quickly enough, she needn't worry about Israel Drake again.

Phoenix looked up. She was so far from everything, there was not even a single streetlight to mar the stark beauty of the stars and the blackness of the night sky beyond. Her breath caught; she felt minuscule, a speck in the cosmos.

What business did Drake have to claim to be the Conduit when there was the entire universe?

She closed her eyes, thanking whoever or whatever was looking out for her that she'd made it this far. One of the straps of her sandals seemed about to break, but she still had miles to walk. Turning toward her right—if her memory was correct, that direction would be the closest town—Phoenix kept walking.

After another long stretch, the sun began to rise, and she guessed it must be close to five in the morning by now. With the light brightening the sky, she could finally tell which way was east. She'd been walking south all night, but she still had no idea how close a town, or even a farmhouse, might be. The best thing she could do would be to stay on this paved road, choosing wider, more dangerous, roads as the options presented themselves. She just hoped she wasn't walking farther into the wilderness.

The sun rose over the mountains in the east, but another light shone through the dawn to the north. From the direction Phoenix had come.

As it drew closer, she realized she was looking at headlights.

The car slowed even as Phoenix's heart sped up. Was this Drake coming after her?

Briefly, she considered diving into the tall weeds on the side of the road, but she had almost certainly already been seen by whoever was driving. The road was straight and flat in this stretch, and there was nowhere to hide.

She swallowed hard and hoped for the best as she turned to face the oncoming car.

It was an older Chevy, at least a decade old, a faded, smoky blue color. Phoenix's heart leapt when she realized that it wasn't one of the vehicles she recognized from the compound. Waving wildly, she stepped a little bit into the road to encourage the driver to slow down.

This was it.

Her real chance to escape.

The car slowed to a stop right next to her, straddling the center line some in an effort to give her safe distance. The driver was an older man, wearing a newsboy cap that reminded her of her grandfather; the woman in the passenger seat, his wife, presumably, was about the same age.

"Hello, dear," the woman said carefully. "Do you need help?"

Phoenix nodded, spluttering, "Yes. Please. Yes. Can you give me a ride to—to the closest town?"

"Where are you headed?" the man asked gruffly.

"I don't know. Maybe—I need to call my family, but I don't have . . . It's a long story," she finished, dejected.

The woman turned to look at her husband, who shrugged before returning his gaze to the road ahead. When the woman turned back to Phoenix, she offered a gentle smile.

"Get in, dear. We'll see that you get what you need."

"Thank you."

Phoenix opened the backdoor and sank into the leather seat. Her muscles ached from walking all night; her feet were bruised and cut from all the miles; her head pounded from dehydration. But all that was okay. She had found help.

"What's your name?"

"Phoenix," she gasped out automatically, before catching herself. "No, wait. Actually—"

The older woman looked at her curiously, her expression a mix of pity and judgment. Phoenix knew perfectly well that this couple most likely assumed she was on drugs of some kind.

"I'm sorry. I've been called Phoenix for the last year; it's what I'm used to. My real name is Jacqueline. Would you call me Jacqueline, please?"

Tears welled up as she let herself hope for the first time in a long time.

"Jacqueline," the woman repeated. "Like the first lady."

Phoenix—Jacqueline—nodded, the tears spilling down her cheeks. She couldn't find the words to thank this woman for the small kindness of seeing her, of hearing her.

"Would you like something to drink, dear?" the woman continued. "Cola? Water? We could get you coffee? What do you like?"

"I . . ." Jacqueline stumbled.

She searched for who she used to be, tried to remember what her life had been like before Israel Drake had controlled every aspect. What did she like to drink? It had been so long since she'd even been given a choice.

"That's all right, dear," the woman said. "You have time to decide. We have about twenty minutes before we reach town, and then we can see what's what. All right?"

Phoenix nodded fervently, overcome and grateful and scared, but finally free.

Inbox Zero

On the last day of Randy's life, he finally reached inbox zero.

This had been a New Year's resolution of his for, oh, approximately twenty years? How long had he had an email address? But it was only in the last five months that he'd taken it seriously, setting his alarm and making himself spend at least an hour every single morning sorting and deleting and responding and deleting before getting to anything else required of his job.

On the last day of Randy's life, he arrived at his cubicle office job an hour and a half early, working off the clock to take care of all these emails, all these requests from other people who had been hounding him for months and longer.

After all these weeks of self-inflicted pressure and extra work hours, he reached inbox zero at precisely 9:44 a.m.

Hardly believing this moment to be real, Randy pushed his chair back from his desk and stared intently at his empty inbox. He had managed to edit his folders down to just under forty different categories. Some of those folders held still-unread missives, but such that he only needed to keep them for his records, not to learn whatever was inside them. Since he'd begun this project in earnest, he had deleted about ten thousand emails each week, and frankly that was being conservative given that new messages continued to come in each day. And on top of all this, he had unsubscribed from no fewer than thirty-five different newsletters, still leaving a dozen or so different companies and contacts on whose lists he needed to stay in order to keep up with his competition and the rest of the industry.

It had been day after day, week after week, of a million tiny decisions, a million little clicks of his mouse. Most choices were easy to make, but the constant wearing down of his willpower made every day a victory of seeing that glaring number of unread emails get a little bit smaller.

Looking around the office that morning, Randy wondered if any of his coworkers had noticed his accomplishment. His sigh of deeply felt pleasure. His blank, white, empty inbox. His several feet of distance from his keyboard, indicating the lack of an immediate task to respond to.

He could almost cry with relief.

But, no, everyone else had their heads down typing or were talking on the phone or walking to the printer and otherwise not noticing this momentous achievement that Randy had been working toward for months.

His chest felt suddenly tight; a reaction, he assumed, to coming down from the adrenaline rush of deleting that very last message. He tried taking a deep breath, tried getting used to this feeling of doneness that had eluded him his entire career. It would be a while, he thought, before this lack of pressing backlog felt normal to him.

He didn't know how he had ended up in what was essentially an "email job." Randy had gone to college for creative writing. Poetry, specifically. Even twenty-eight years later, he was still rather pleased with the chapbook he had put together for his senior thesis. But that summer following graduation he had needed something to pay the bills while he built up his portfolio and submitted to literary magazines on nights and weekends. And then, by simple virtue of not being terrible and keeping his mouth shut, he had managed to climb the corporate ladder, more or less.

All those years later, he was still stuck at a desk in one of those dreaded open plans with cubicles practically on top of each other and virtually no agency to even decide how he was going to spend his eight hours there.

Outlook refreshed and three emails popped in, their bolded subject lines demanding Randy's immediate attention.

His heart hammered. He lurched forward and tried to skim their contents as quickly as possible and get rid of them. There were so many other ways he wanted to be spending his time, but rushing through this task seemed like the only real solution.

Randy had told himself that once he finally reached inbox zero, he would already be in the habit of waking up to come to work early and he could then pivot to spending that extra morning hour writing poetry. That was what he most wished to be doing with his time, with his brain. In the almost three decades since he'd left college he'd had a total of four poems published, most of those in the first couple years. What had started out as encouraging momentum for his literary career had turned into thin hopes of one published poem per decade.

But today was the day. All of that focus and—

Two more emails popped in.

Randy growled in frustration, loud enough to draw a concerned look from Mary, who sat just across the aisle from him.

One of these emails could be filed away for his records, but the other he needed to answer, explaining to his boss's boss—again, with supporting links and Wikipedia stats—exactly why it was a big deal that Gary Vee had retweeted that YouTuber's review of their company's CRM software.

As his fingers stabbed at the keys as quickly as he could get the salient facts down, he again felt his chest tightening. His breath was short, as the fear of more emails coming in while he was busy with this one descended on him.

What he really needed, Randy thought, was a day off. A day to not think about emails at all. To maybe even think about poems again. Though he wanted to celebrate and take a break to enjoy this accomplishment, he also knew that if he walked away from his desk he would come back to another four or five emails at least. If he took a whole day off, then he'd be looking at something close to seventy, eighty emails—a hundred? At least half of which he could delete, sure, but it still took time. And if he started to fall behind, he was afraid he'd never catch up again.

By the time he'd sent the email about the retweet, three more emails had flown in to take its place.

Where before Randy had wanted to cry from relief, now he wanted to cry from the futility of this Sisyphean task that life had set before him.

He knew, in theory, that if he somehow managed to pay his bills publishing poetry—yes, an absurd conceit, but *in theory*—there would still be emails.

But surely it would be nothing like this.

How could there be, in the history of the world, another job like this? Unending email, demands for attention, futile repetitive micro dopamine hits that somehow filled an eight-hour shift, day after day, year after year.

Five more emails. All at once. Including one from his direct supervisor about scheduling a meeting for his annual review the following week. Which meant he would need to check his calendar against other client calls. Which was another minute at least that he was not actively monitoring the inbox, and who knew how many more could come in during that time?

He rolled his shoulders back, trying to loosen the increasing tightness that seemed to have his rib cage in a giant clamp. His vision was going spotty. Randy told himself he just needed to calm down. Breathe a little. Another email was not going to be the end of the world.

But then he remembered how very much of his personal time and effort he had invested into reaching this point, and he refused to let the obnoxious capitalist system of 24/7 availability win. He would not let these emails bury him.

His hand shook as he dragged the mouse to file away the emails, to delete more emails, to type out a quick response. Having even more trouble catching his breath, Randy began to fear that he *had* to take a break, that he would be forced to walk away from his computer and allow whatever emails were going to come in to bombard him upon his eventual return.

As soon as the final email was taken care of and he was back to zero, Randy forced himself to swivel in his chair, away from the computer screen. He closed his eyes. His chest was in even more pain than it had been before, and that pain was now spreading down his left arm.

Randy attempted to stand, collapsed to his knees on the thin, industrial blue rug, and fell forward.

On the last day of Randy's life, his final thought—as his heart ultimately succumbed to the lack of blood and oxygen, and seized in his chest—was of the massive expense calling an ambulance would be, and the desperate hope that the hospital would not be emailing their invoices.

Author's Note

I've moved homes more than a dozen times in my life. I've lived in five different states and flown to multiple countries and quit I-don't-know-how-many jobs and ended several relationships.

Sometimes the solution *is* running away.

My two short story collections are not put together the way most traditional authors compile their own collections. I don't submit stories to lit mags in advance (though I should / will in the future). Instead I start collecting vague ideas for stories, and when I start to see a pattern or through line, I focus in on that theme. Once I know the theme, I brainstorm a few dozen ideas and premises. And then I see what sticks. There is probably another 20k words of first draft stories still sitting on my harddrive that didn't make the final cut.

In the case of *Flight,* the themes of these stories are about leaving home. Leaving your comfort zone, leaving a relationship or situation or expectation. Most of what I write also looks at the themes of secrecy, information, and how wielding each translates into power. For example, in "Give Artie My Love" the main character is regularly dropping hints of what she knows in an attempt to destabilize the person she's speaking to.

The characters in these stories are all either flying from something, or flying to something. When I first envisioned this collection, I assumed that there would be at least a couple of travel stories in it. Somehow, though, those ideas ended up to be far less compelling than a story about someone standing up to their spouse, or someone pushing through inertia to go for a run.

I am a sucker for those quiet, Oscar-bait movies, and those are the kind of stories I want to tell. Even the smallest decision can be the domino that sets off a whole life change.

Let this collection be a reminder to you that you don't actually have to stay in any situation you do not want to. One thing that I've said more than once is that the only decision in life that is *actually* permanent is having kids. Everything else you can undo if you really want to.

Don't forget. You can leave whenever you want.

Amy Teegan
April 2025

Selected Story Notes

Stories about leaving home:

"GIVE ARTIE MY LOVE" — Thank you to Spencer for the title of this story. In fact, thank you to Spencer for most of the story titles. I am terrible at that. In my draft, this was just called 'voicemails'.

It's an epistolary story, told via transcripts of voice memos left by one character to another.

It was (very) loosely inspired by a conversation I had with an old boyfriend (kind of), not long after he got married. We were just catching up, and as I'm asking questions about his new wife (and life in general), I realize that not only has he not told her a single thing about his past that I was part of, but he also hasn't asked her any questions about her own past. It was … so strange. I still don't understand.

But it got me thinking about what someone significantly more unhinged than me would do in a similar situation.

(Let's be honest—that's where a lot of my story ideas come from.)

Epistolary stories (and I have two trunk novels written in a similar way) are always fun because I get to lean on my theater-kid past. Step into the character and just let the improvisation flow. In these cases the first draft always *flies* by.

It's the revision, making it a coherent and well-structured story, that takes time.

But the first person, unhinged manipulating voice is *so* fun to write.

"PASTOR MATT" — This is one of my favorite stories in the collection, but given that I grew up in an evangelical church and still am friends with a lot of those people, I expect this story to be the most controversial. Though personally I did not experience anything like this, I could name probably 6 or 8 friends off the top of my head who did.

It's written in 1st person plural (we / our), which (in my opinion) is essential for the interpretation of it. This is a universal experience for girls within patriarchal systems. Period.

"CONVERSE" — This is one of Spencer's favorite stories in the collection, and ended up much more poignant and sweet than I had anticipated. I'd had a vague idea of a premise (changing habits, learning to be a runner), but nothing more until the 2024 Summer Olympics. During those two weeks I happened to be traveling with one of my best friends and she was *super* excited to be watching the games whenever we had a chance. That one small detail helped tie together everything I was trying to do with this story, and without it, I probably would not have included it in the collection. (Thanks, Kam!)

"THE DIVINE CURRENT" — This is the longest story in the book, which is a bit of an accomplishment for me. I tend to both underwrite in general, and gravitate toward little vignettes instead of full-blown stories. But I found that the world-building of this story (a young woman escaping a cult) required more time and detail than I usually spend.

The cult (fictional) in question is part of the backstory of a series of books I plan to write, so it was both worth the time I took to make Future Amy's life easier, and far more interesting to me than if this was a story unattached to anything else.

In CliftonStrengths parlance, I have high Context, which means knowing the backstory and full world (and context) for things helps me write better. (This is also why I don't really write speculative fiction. Having to *create* the context for my story feels like a huge project. I have plenty to work with in just our real world.)

I'm not sure how much of the cult will actually show up on the page when I go to write that other series, so I'm glad I took the time with it now.

Acknowledgments

Thank you to Spencer as always for letting me talk your ear off about all of these stories. You helped me brainstorm broad strokes and fine-tune details. I appreciate that you are unwaveringly my biggest fan and also willing to reformat all my ellipses.

Thank you to family for loving me despite my weird author habits and threats to constantly put you in a book. Reminder that this book is fiction. I didn't actually do any of these things, please don't worry too much.

Thank you to my author friends—OneMind and ALAS and VKF and everyone who has offered me a tidbit of advice. Your support and tactics help me pay my bills in other ways, so I can take the time to write these literary stories that fewer readers are looking for. My life would be utterly different if I had never joined the indie author community.

Thank you to KKM for listening to me yap about every subject under the sun. Among other things, you gave me the idea for the PhD subject in one of these stories. You've been a pillar of my life for well over a decade now and I'm so grateful.

Thank you to you, the reader, for buying this book, for reading this far, for reviews and comments, and for being with me on this journey.

Also by Amy Teegan

No Day Like Today

Poison: Stories

Deep: A Story of Family and Fear

About the Author

Amy Teegan is a reader, writer and traveler currently living in central Pennsylvania.

Follow her at amyteegan.com.

www.ingramcontent.com/pod-product-compliance
Lightning Source LLC
Chambersburg PA
CBHW021714190726
48289CB00008B/2522